Too Young To Die

Alida E. Young

For my aunts, Marianne Cooper and Margo Jones

And to my editor and dear friend, Gwen

Special thanks to Robert Anastas, Founder and Executive Director of SADD; Diane Parrish, ICU/CCU/PCU, Head Nurse of Hi-Desert Medical Center; Loma Linda University Medical Center; Steve Proctor, Ohio Department of Highway Safety; and to Terri Dicknieder, Linda Carpenter, and Paul J. Kingsley.

Cover photo by
The Photographic Illustrators

Published by Willowisp Press, Inc.
401 E. Wilson Bridge Road, Worthington, Ohio 43085

Copyright ©1987 by Willowisp Press, Inc.

Printed in the United States of America

10 9 8 7 6 5 4 3 2

ISBN 0-87406-236-5

One

"**SHANE!**" Robin screamed. "Get up! Get up!"

Just as Shane McAllister had caught the football, he'd been tackled. He lay on the ground for a second, then got up slowly.

Robin sighed with relief. The crowd roared.

As the team headed back into the huddle, Robin Nichols watched Shane walk to the bench. She nudged her friend's arm and nearly made Cheryl drop her hotdog. "Cheryl, does Shane look like he's limping?"

"He'd better be okay," Mike said, trying to see down to the sidelines. "Without Shane we don't have a chance of winning."

"We'd better win," Bob said. "I heard there's a scout from one of the big colleges looking at Troy Haliburton."

"I'll bet they're taking a long look at Shane, too," Jackie said. "He's the best wide receiver

3

Woodbridge has had in years." She leaned past Cheryl and grinned at Robin. "And he's the best looking one, too."

Robin couldn't argue with that. Shane was dark-haired, brown-eyed, tall, and as good-looking as any TV or movie star. And I'm wearing his jacket, she thought.

Robin, Cheryl, Jackie, Mike, and Bob had come to the game together. Jackie and Cheryl were Robin's best friends. Bob and Mike were Shane's best friends. The guys were all on the track team and belonged to the same clubs. Robin liked both Bob and Mike, but they weren't as much fun as Shane. He was special. Robin absently ran her fingers over the gold track letter.

A full moon with a silvery halo seemed to be perched over the top of the stands. The October air was brisk, with a feeling of rain. The aluminum bench was cold, and Robin drew Shane's jacket tighter around her neck.

The football game between Woodbridge High and Benson High, their crosstown rival, was the biggest game of the season. And right now Benson was winning 13 to 10. I just hope Shane's all right, Robin thought.

One of the cheerleaders blew his whistle to get everyone's attention in the Woodbridge section of the stands. Robin jumped up and joined in the Viking yell.

Robin spotted Shane running back onto the field. He didn't seem to be limping now and Robin breathed a prayer of thanks. The crowd screamed as the team lined up for the next play.

It was Woodbridge's ball on Benson's thirty-five yard line, and there was less than a minute left on the clock. Troy Haliburton, the quarterback, took the ball from the center, rolled out, and drew back his arm to throw. The crowd was yelling, "Troy! Troy! Touchdown!"

Robin glanced downfield. Shane was wide open, waiting for the pass. But Troy hesitated too long, and the defense rushed him. He tried to scramble, but lost his footing in the damp grass.

A groan went up as he was sacked.

Woodbridge was backed up to the forty-nine yard line.

The crowd was yelling so loud that Troy put his hand up for quiet. This time he took the ball and stepped into the pocket. Again, Shane had gotten away from his defender. Troy passed to Shane, but the throw was high. Shane leaped into the air and made an impossible catch. He escaped two tacklers, and raced into the end zone for a touchdown just as time ran out, ending the game.

The Woodbridge side of the stands went crazy. Robin hugged Cheryl and Jackie. Mike and Bob were clapping everybody on the back.

"Shane did it! We won. We Won!"

The Woodbridge kicker put the icing on the cake by making the extra point. As the team ran off the field, Robin saw Shane look up into the stands where he knew she would be sitting. He gave a victory sign.

A surge of happiness and pride filled her. She wanted to shout, It's me he's waving to. I'm Shane's girl.

* * * * *

Robin dug through her closet for her other boot. She tossed out shoes, fallen hangers, and dirty clothes.

"You look like a dog hunting for a buried bone." It was her father standing at the door of her room. "I keep expecting the health department to quarantine us."

He was grinning, but Robin knew he was only half joking. He usually referred to her room as Robin's Nest. She'd had a pet canary once and knew what he meant. Its cage had always been a mess.

"I think we should have a yard sale and sell

all this junk," he said and spread his arms to include her stuffed animals and collection of hats.

She pretended to think he was serious. "But, Daddy, I cleaned my room last Saturday. I think we have gremlins and one of them stole my boot. How can a boot just disappear?"

He looked around the huge room and shook his head. "A herd of elephants could disappear in here."

Even her friends kidded her about the disaster area. It was a great room, though. It was large enough to hold not only her bedroom furniture, but also a couch, a stereo, and her collections, with enough space left to dance in. The room was a hangout for Robin and her friends.

"Robin, honey," her father said, "I didn't come in to give you a hard time about your room. I wanted to tell you that I won't be able to pick you and Shane up after the carnival. I just got called into work. I have no idea when I'll get back."

Her father was a technical writer for Woodbridge Aeronautics. He wrote manuals for pilots to use. He was always getting calls to work on Saturdays, spoiling plans for skiing or camping or going to baseball games.

"That's okay," Robin said. "Mom can—"

"No, she has to take a deposition this afternoon. And the lawyer's office is clear at the other end of the county."

Robin's mother was a court reporter, only she took depositions for civil cases. Her father held out two dollars. "Here's money for the bus. Just be sure to get home before dark."

"Don't worry. I have to babysit tonight."

He bent down and kissed her on the top of the head. "Have a good time. I'll see you later."

She nodded. I'm lucky, she thought. Cheryl and Jackie are always talking about how they get mad at their parents. Mine never hassle me, and we do a lot of fun things together. Maybe it's because I'm an only child. Cheryl had told Robin it was awful to have a sister, especially a younger one. She and her sister were always fighting. And they had to share a room. Robin grinned to herself. If I had a sister, where would she put her stuff? Robin went back to looking for her boot.

"Robin," her mother called, "Shane's here. Are you ready?"

Robin clumped to the door and called, "Tell him I'll be right there. Mom, have you seen my other brown boot?"

"Did you look under your bed?"

8

Robin got on her knees and fished under the brass bed. Out came a sweater that had been missing for a month, an overdue library book, a baseball cap, and the boot. Quickly, she pulled it on, then hung the cap on the wall next to an orange hard hat. Her Uncle Burt had gotten her started on the hat collection when he was working in construction. Now one wall was filled.

Robin had every kind of hat imaginable, from a Greek fisherman's cap, which she wore often, to a cowboy hat that a real cowboy from Wyoming had given her. Shane's favorite was a sombrero that her father had bought in Mexico. Sometimes when the kids were listening to music in Robin's room, Shane would sit on the floor with his knees drawn up to his chest and the sombrero pulled down over his face.

She took one last look in the mirror and retied the green scarf. The new white sweater and matching knit cap looked good, she thought. And she liked the way her brown hair curled up around the cap. Today was going to be a perfect day. Whenever she was with Shane, it was a perfect day.

She hurried out to the living room where her mother and Shane were talking.

"It's beautiful," her mother said as she sniffed a single white rose. "Thank you very much, Shane."

"It's no big thing, Mrs. Nichols. It just came from our garden," he said. "It's the last one of the season."

No wonder her parents liked him. He was always doing unexpected things like that. Once he'd brought her mother an African violet for her collection, which included nearly every kind of plant in the world. Her father was always kidding about living in a jungle. But he was a collector, too. His study was full of model airplanes.

Shane turned and grinned at Robin. "You took so long, we thought maybe you'd gotten lost under your bed."

Robin ignored his teasing. "Are you ready?" she asked. "We're supposed to meet the rest of the kids at one o'clock."

"Not so fast," her mother said. "You haven't cleaned up the lunch dishes."

"Mom, we'll be late."

Her mother just pointed toward the kitchen.

"Come on, I'll help you," Shane said. "It won't take long. I'm an expert at washing dishes—especially when there's an automatic dishwasher."

Shane helped Robin clear the table and load the dishwasher. They both reached for a glass at the same time, and their hands touched.

Neither moved. They stood there silently looking at each other, then he gave her that smile of his that always turned her knees to melted butter.

"You look great," he said. "The green scarf makes your eyes look even greener."

"Thanks," she whispered drawing a sinkful of water. She never tired of looking at him. All his feelings showed on his face. She always knew if he were happy or sad or felt sorry for someone. Right now, his brown eyes were telling her how much he cared about her.

Shane was fifteen, a year older than Robin. He lived on the street behind her. They had known each other ever since she was in the first grade. For years their parents had borrowed lawnmowers and extra chairs for company and cups of sugar. But last winter their two families had gone skiing together at Lake Tahoe. After that, she and Shane had started jogging together every morning. And things had been different between them.

Shane gently touched her nose with a soapy finger. He moved closer and bent his head. She closed her eyes, waiting for his kiss.

A sound at the door startled her. She drew back and began to busily clatter dishes.

Her mother came into the kitchen and filled a vase with water for the rose. "Robin, you'd better take a raincoat or an umbrella. The weatherman is predicting rain by late afternoon."

"I'll finish here, Shane. Would you mind getting my red jacket from my room?"

"Are you sure I can find it in The Hole?" he asked.

She made a face at him and flipped him with the dish towel. "Don't get smart," Robin told him. "I think it's hanging over my guitar."

"Why? Is the guitar cold?"

She groaned at the bad joke. "It keeps the dust off."

"That's the worst excuse I've ever heard," Shane said. "If I'm not back in an hour, send out a search party."

Robin finished wiping off the counters and emptied the garbage. Shane was sure taking a long time. She went to the hall and called, "Can't you find it?"

"I'm coming, I'm coming," Shane answered. "You need a tour guide to find your way around that room."

When he came out, he helped Robin into the jacket, then he slipped into his own jeans jacket.

Robin's mother followed them to the front door. "Have a good time. And please be home before dark."

* * * * *

Woodbridge, in Northern California, wasn't a very large town. It had two high schools, two movie theaters, and dozens of pizza parlors. Every October, Woodbridge High had a carnival in the gymnasium. Both Robin and Shane had helped set up booths. Shane had to be in the Hunk-Dunk booth from one-thirty to two. When they were buying their tickets, Robin grinned at him. "I'm going to save most of my tickets so I can try to dunk you."

"Who's worried?" he mocked.

"I've been practicing," she said smugly.

Making their way through a crowd of noisy little kids, they looked for their friends. "I don't see them," Robin said.

"It's not one o'clock yet. They'll find us. Come on." Shane pulled Robin by the hand over to a dart-throwing booth.

"Hi, Tim," Shane said to the boy behind the counter. "Let's have some darts." He looked at the prizes. "There. That's what I want to win," he said, pointing to a pink hat with a long green feather. "For your collection, Robin."

Robin laughed when he missed the first throw. The second try was closer.

When he finally won the hat, he handed it to

her. "Why don't you wear it?"

"You're kidding! I won't wear that ridiculous thing. It goes on my wall."

"And after all the work I went to." He pretended to look hurt. "Aw, come on, Birdie, put it on."

"Shane McAllister, don't call me that." Ever since he'd heard her Uncle Burt call her Birdie, he'd called her that to tease her. "Just wait until I get you at the dunk tank. I'm going to hit the bull's-eye so many times that you're going to live in that water."

"I'm really worried, Ace."

"Hey, Shane, Robin."

They turned to see Cheryl and Bob over by the cider stand. Jackie and Mike were there, too. Shane and Robin waved and hurried to join their friends.

"Hi, guys," Robin and Shane said at the same time.

Jackie laughed and pointed to the pink hat. "Robin, where'd you get that dumb hat? That's the worst one yet."

Robin glanced at Shane. "Shane won it for my collection," she said.

They all ordered cider and then headed for the dunk tank. On the way, they passed a little boy who was crying. Shane stopped and asked, "What's wrong? Are you lost?"

The boy shook his head and cried even harder.

"Oh, come on, Shane," Mike said. "The kid probably broke his balloon."

"You guys go on," Shane told everyone. "I'll be right there."

Robin stayed with Shane. He knelt down beside the boy. "Anything I can do to help?" Shane asked.

The boy was crying so hard he couldn't answer Shane for a bit. Then between sobs he choked out, "I lost all my tickets. My big brother's going to be mad."

Shane fished into his pockets. "I have some. Want to come over to the dunking booth and try to put me into the water?"

Leave it to Shane to stop and help a little kid, Robin thought.

"I have to wait for my brother," the boy said.

"Well, here." Shane gave the boy most of his tickets. Robin gave him some, too.

"Gee, thanks," the boy said, a smile replacing the tears. "This is more tickets than I had to start with."

Robin and Shane caught up with the others at the dunking booth. While Shane went to get into his swimming trunks, they all watched Troy Haliburton on the dunk seat. Troy was tall, blond, and still tan from spending the summer at the beach. In swim trunks he looked even more muscular than he did on the football field. Dozens of girls were waiting to dunk him.

"Isn't he gorgeous?" Cheryl whispered to Robin. "Talk about a hunk to dunk."

"Sorry, everybody," Troy said. "My time's up."

All the girls waiting in line squealed and yelled. "I didn't get a turn yet."

"Come on, Birthday Boy," a senior called to Troy. "Let's get this party on the road."

Troy grinned and left. There was a lot of groaning and booing until Shane walked out and climbed onto the dunk seat. Shane wasn't as big or muscular as Troy, but he was just as good-looking. The line of girls got even longer.

Robin watched while Mike and Bob dunked Shane several times. Shane always came up laughing. Jackie and Cheryl tried but missed. When it was Robin's turn, Shane yelled, "You'll never get me!"

Robin took careful aim and hit the mark squarely in the center. "Gotcha!"

Shane came up spitting water. "Lucky shot, Ace. You can't do it again."

"You'd better close your mouth," Robin called. She threw two more times but missed.

16

"Robin, we're going to the Bop-booth," Cheryl said. "We'll meet you there."

"Okay. I'll wait for Shane to be finished here, then we'll join you."

When Shane's time was up and he was dressed, they joined their friends at the Bop-booth.

Robin and Shane hit each other with pillows. After a dozen times, Robin yelled, "Stop! I'm getting a headache."

"Me, too," Shane said. "I don't know why we're paying money to do this."

"Yeah," Mike called. "You can beat each other up at home."

"Let's go to some of the other booths," Jackie suggested. "I want Mike to win me a stuffed bear."

The group went from booth to booth until they had an armload of balloons, jewelry, and junk.

Shane had won the only good prize. "It's yours," he said to Robin and gave her the adorable, cuddly stuffed white bunny. It had a smile just like Shane's.

"Oh, I love him," she said. "He reminds me of you."

Shane twitched his nose. "Old MacDonald had a farm," he sang. "Ee—ay—ee—ay—oh. And on this farm there was a rabbit . . ." He pretended to munch on a carrot.

"You're crazy," Robin told him. "Who ever heard of a rabbit on MacDonald's farm?"

"Who cares about rabbits and farms?" Cheryl said. "I'm starved. Let's get a pizza."

"With everything on it," Bob and Mike said in unison.

"I'm on a diet," Jackie moaned. "Everything here is fattening."

"Leave it to me," Shane told them.

They went to the pizza booth. "Hi, Greg. Hi, Melissa." Shane seemed to know every kid in school. "We want five slices of pizza with everything on it and one diet pizza for Jackie."

"You're a nut, Shane McAllister," Jackie said.

Shane grinned. "But lovable," he said to Jackie.

Robin glanced at her watch. "It's getting late, and I have to babysit this evening."

Cheryl groaned. "I have to be home before dark."

"Me, too," Jackie put in.

"I'm sick of rules." Cheryl made a fist and punched the air. "You'd think we were babies! I want to win a stuffed animal before I leave."

Robin felt lucky. Her parents hardly ever had rules to obey. She'd even worried that maybe her folks didn't care about her. Once she'd asked her parents, "How come you don't give me a bunch of rules like my friends get?"

"Because you've never given us any reason to have to lay down a list of rules," her father had told her. "But just step out of line once, and you'll see how fast you get some rules."

"I have to go," Robin said. "It may be hard to get a bus."

"Yeah," Mike said. "They're always crowded after one of the Jr. College football games."

"Robin, call me tomorrow," Cheryl said.

"Come on over later," Mike said to Shane.

They all waved good-bye, and Robin and Shane made their way to the exit.

Outside, the air felt cold and damp, as if it might rain any minute. "I hope my rabbit doesn't get wet," she said.

"Here, wrap him in this," he said as he pulled off his jacket.

"Shane, you're crazy. You'll freeze."

"Come, on, I'll beat you to the bus stop. That'll warm me up."

"Wait for me!" Robin yelled. Dodging kids and bikes, she caught up with him at the sidewalk. At the bus stop it started to drizzle, almost sleeting it was so cold. There was a big crowd ahead of them, so they weren't able to get on the first two buses. "I didn't realize it got dark so early now," Robin said. "Mom's going to bawl me out."

"We'll make the next one," Shane told her. He shivered. "You're right, though. It is cold out here."

The rain was coming down harder now. "Put on your jacket," she said.

"Only if you wear the pink hat."

"I wouldn't be caught dead in that silly thing. People will think I'm nuts."

"Who cares what other people think. It'll look great on you. The green feather matches your eyes."

"Shane, I won't wear that dumb—"

A screech of tires stopped her. She turned to see a car skid on the rain-slippery street and jump the curb. Car lights blinded her for a moment, then she saw the driver's mouth open in a silent scream.

Shane pushed her aside. She crashed against the bench and fell. Gravel cut into her arms and knees.

"Shane!" she screamed.

Grinding metal. Moaning. Pain. The taste of blood. Then blackness, blessed blackness.

Two

"SHANE, I won't wear that dumb ..." The screech of tires filled her ears. She saw the car bearing down on them, but couldn't move. Blinding light—Shane pushing her out of the way. Falling. Someone screaming. Pain . . . .

"Shane!" She struggled up from the darkness. It was a dream, a terrible nightmare. "Shane!"

"Robin, it's all right." Her mother held her hand and whispered softly, "It's all right, baby. You're all right."

And she was a little girl again with her mother beside her bed, telling her that she'd had a bad dream. She opened her eyes and saw her mother's face. "Oh, Mom, I had an awful—" She stopped as she noticed that she was in a strange room. And there was a tube attached to her arm. She jolted up in bed. Her body screamed with pain, and she sank back against the pillow. "Mom! It wasn't a dream.

21

There was a crash—Shane! Where's Shane?"

"Robin, you mustn't get excited. Lie down, honey. Nurse!" her mother shouted. The sound of her mother's voice was too sharp, too alarmed.

The nurse came in and added something to Robin's IV. "She'll calm down in a minute," the nurse said.

"I want to see Shane." Robin tried to sit up, but her body felt too heavy. "Let me see Shane!"

"Later, honey." Her mother stroked her forehead. "Right now, you need to rest. I'll be right here when you wake up."

Robin felt drowsy. Soon her arm and head grew heavy. The pain in her stomach eased a little. "I have—to—see—" Her eyelids fluttered shut.

* * * * *

She awakened slowly to the sound of her parents' voices.

"I feel so sorry for the McAllisters. I just thank God that Robin—" Her mother's voice broke.

"I'll never forgive myself for not picking them up at the carnival," her father said. "My job isn't that important."

Robin opened her eyes to see her mom and dad sitting near the bed. She saw the worry and tiredness on their faces. "Mom? Daddy?" she said weakly. "Where's Shane? He was in front of me—I saw him—"

"Ssh, ssh, it's all right." Her father pulled his chair close to the bed and took her hand.

They were lying to her, she thought. She had heard Shane's scream and seen him fall. "He's dead, and you're not telling me!" Her voice rose. "He's dead and I'll never see him again!"

"Honey, he's seriously hurt," her father told her quietly. "But he's alive. He's in the intensive care unit."

"I want to see him. I have to see him." She tried to raise up, but her father gently pushed her back.

"Not yet. You have to stay quiet. The doctor will be in soon."

Robin noticed the light from the window. "What time is it? How long have I been here?"

Her dad looked at his watch. "It's nine in the morning."

They looked so tired, she thought. Her father needed a shave. Her mother's eye makeup was smudged, her brown hair disarrayed. They were still wearing the same clothes they'd worn the day before.

Vaguely now, she remembered being wheeled into an elevator, having people in masks working over her, seeing machines and needles. Her abdomen felt tender. There were scrapes and bandages on her arms and legs. A tube ran from her hand to a clear plastic bag hanging on a metal stand. She ran her fingers over the bracelet with her name on it. "Am . . . am I okay?"

"You've had a lot of tests," her mother said. "You don't have any broken bones. The doctor will be in soon to tell us when you can go home."

"What about Shane?"

"Dr. Webber will tell—"

"Is somebody talking about me?" A tall, heavyset man in a green shirt and pants came into the room. "Well, I'm glad to see you're awake, young lady." He glanced at a clipboard. "How do you feel?"

"I don't care about me. I have to know if Shane—"

"Shane McAllister is the boy who was in the accident with Robin," her mother said.

The doctor nodded. "I just came from ICU. His condition has stabilized, but he's still in a coma."

"Coma?" Robin asked.

"There is swelling in the brain. It causes

24

profound unconsciousness, like a very, very deep sleep."

"But he'll be all right, won't he?"

"We have no way of knowing," the doctor said. "We're doing everything we can for him."

Robin's eyes filled with tears. "May I see him?"

"I want you to stay quiet for a day or two. You have an injured pancreas." He touched her abdomen, and she flinched. "Is it tender?"

"It's not so bad," Robin said. "Some of these scrapes on my arms and legs hurt worse."

"You rest today. I'll ask the boy's parents. If it's all right with them, I'll get a nurse to take you in to see your friend tomorrow."

"Thank you, doctor, for taking such good care of our girl," Robin's dad said.

As Dr. Webber started to leave, Robin's mother and father walked out of the room with him. Were they talking about her—or Shane? Robin wondered.

In a moment her parents were back.

"Was he telling me the truth?" she asked them. "Am I going to be okay?"

"Yes, honey. You just need rest," her mother said. "We'll go get some breakfast and be right back."

"I'm kind of hungry, too." Robin tried to

joke so they wouldn't worry about her. "This sure is some crummy hotel. When do I get room service around here?"

"I'll tell the nurse—"

Her mother stopped as a uniformed man came into the room. "Mr. and Mrs. Nichols?" he asked.

Her father nodded. "Yes. What is it?"

"Patrolman Carson." The policeman held out his ID. "I'd like to question your daughter about the accident." he said.

"Can't this wait?" her father asked, his voice sounding angry. "First it was reporters, then an insurance adjuster. Now the police. You can see she's in no condition to talk about it yet."

"We'll try not to take too long, but the sooner we talk to her the better. It's easy to forget the details."

"It's okay, Dad," Robin said. "I—I don't mind." She turned to the policeman. "Do you know who hit us? Was he hurt?"

"Not a scratch. His name is Troy Haliburton."

"Troy! He was at the carnival. It happened so fast—did he skid on the wet pavement?"

"He's been charged with drunk driving," Carson said grimly.

"But he's on the football team. He doesn't even drink," Robin said.

"It was his birthday. Apparently he left the carnival early and went celebrating. He was on his way home. Did you see the car?"

She shook her head. "Not really. Just at the very last second. I don't even know what color it was."

"What direction did it come from?"

"I guess from across Broadway. We were waiting for a bus."

"Can you remember what happened?"

"I really didn't see anything." Robin closed her eyes and leaned back. She shuddered as the memory of the crash came back. "The sound—it was awful."

"That's enough, Officer," her father said. "It's too hard on her."

"We have one eyewitness who saw everything. We just wanted to be sure she hadn't seen something different. Thank you." Patrolman Carson smiled for the first time. "You're a lucky young woman."

"What about the Haliburton boy?" her father asked. "What's going to happen to him?"

"Probably not much. He's a minor. He's already been remanded to the custody of his parents." The cop sounded bitter.

When they were gone, her father banged his fist against the windowsill. "I should have come after you and Shane."

Robin was thinking about Troy. Troy—star athlete, an A student, the best looking guy in Woodbridge High. Most of the girls she knew had a crush on him. She could hardly believe it had been Troy she'd seen through the windshield.

Sudden anger filled her. Troy didn't have a scratch on him, and Shane was in a coma. It wasn't right. It just wasn't fair.

* * * * *

The next morning Robin's mother stopped at the hospital on her way to work. She brought Robin's robe and some makeup.

"Well, you look better," her mother said. She kissed Robin's forehead. "How do you feel?"

"Pretty good. But they woke me up practically in the middle of the night to get washed for breakfast. Then it was two hours before I ate."

A nurse came into the room. "Mrs. Nichols, a Pat Erickson from the radio station would like to talk to your daughter. Is it all right?"

"Oh, I don't know." Robin's mother frowned doubtfully. "Are you up to it, honey?"

"I guess so, but what can I tell him?"

"She's a her, not a him. And she's a good reporter," the nurse said. "She does human interest stories."

Robin shrugged. "I guess it's okay. Anyway, there's not much else to do in this place."

"I'll go talk to her first, Robin" her mother said.

Robin could hear them talking in the hall, then they came into the room.

The reporter came over to the bed. "Hi," she said, "I'm Pat Erickson. If you don't mind, I'd like to talk to you for a few minutes."

"Okay, but I don't much like talking about the accident, Miss Erickson."

"Call me Pat. I just want to talk about you and the boy who was hurt. You tell me if you start to get tired."

Pat pulled up a chair. "Mind if I use a tape recorder?" She grinned ruefully. "I have a lousy memory."

The reporter looked to be in her middle twenties. She had a nice smile, with little crinkly lines by her blue eyes. Robin liked her right off.

"Now, just tell me a little about you and the boy—is it Shane McAllister?"

"Yes. I've known him most of my life."

"They live right behind us," Robin's mother put in. "You couldn't ask for a nicer family."

Robin talked easily about Shane—about how everybody liked him—about his great future as an athlete. "But he's not just a jock. He's smart and fun and—well, he's just Shane."

"He sounds like a terrific person," Pat said. "What about the other boy? Troy Haliburton."

"He's just about the most popular guy in school."

"Does he run around with a rough crowd?"

"Troy?" Robin laughed. "He's always been Mister super-straight. I mean, I was really surprised when they said he'd been charged with drunk driving."

Robin stopped. "I don't think I should be talking about him. You should interview him."

"I'd like to, but his family refused to let me see him."

"Well, I hope he gets what he deserves," Robin's mother said. "Something needs to be done about drunk drivers."

"I'm glad to hear you say that, Mrs. Nichols. It's a terrible problem. Did you know that one out of every two people will be in an accident involving a drunk driver at some time in his life?"

"That's incredible," Robin's mother said.

"Yes, it is. More than 25,000 people are killed every year by drunk drivers." Pat leaned forward. Her hands were clenched, her eyes intense. "According to MADD, that's Mothers Against Drunk Driving, nearly 14 teenagers die and 360 are injured every day in alcohol-related deaths. It's a national disgrace, and we should all be trying to fight it." Pat sighed and leaned back. "I'm sorry. I didn't mean to get on my soapbox, but we have to change people's attitudes about drinking."

Robin was stunned by the statistics. "But Troy wasn't a drinker," she said.

"That's what's so awful, Robin. Someone takes a few drinks, gets into a car, and kills or maims someone. So many people's lives are ruined—including the driver. His life will never be the same again."

"Well, I don't have any sympathy for Troy," Robin said. "I hope he's never allowed in a car again."

"Robin, have you ever heard of the organization SADD, Students Against Driving Drunk?"

Robin shook her head no.

"It's a group that tries to get students and the community involved. You know—help change attitudes about drunk driving."

"Sounds like a good idea," Robin said.

"Now isn't the time to talk about it, but when you get back on your feet, give me a call.

You and your friends might be interested in starting a chapter in your school."

Robin's mother spoke up. "That sounds worthwhile." She walked over to the bed and kissed Robin. "Honey, I have to get to work now. Your father and I will be here this evening. You get some rest. You need to get your strength back."

"I will, Mom. Bye."

Pat switched off her recorder and stood up. "I appreciate your talking to me, Robin. I'll let you know when the piece will be aired."

Robin nodded.

"Take care, now. I hope you and your friend are out of the hospital right away."

She was already at the door when Robin asked, "Pat, how come you know so much about drunk driving?"

Robin saw Pat's back stiffen. The reporter didn't turn to look at Robin. "I could have saved my friend's life if I hadn't let him get behind the wheel of a car when he'd been drinking."

Pat turned around then, and Robin saw a glint of tears in her eyes. "We hit a tree. He was killed."

Robin looked down at her hands and realized she was twisting the corner of the sheet. "I should be in a coma, not Shane," she

said almost in a whisper. "He pushed me out
of the way."

* * * * *

After a lunch of broth and strawberry
gelatin, Robin started to get herself ready to
visit Shane. The nurse had removed the tube
from her arm so she could put on her makeup
and brush her hair. Her mother had brought
the fitted traveling case that had a mirror and
small bottles of creams and lotions. When
Robin was little, she had loved to play with
her mother's case. Twice she had sneaked into
her mother's closet and taken the case back to
her own room. She tried all the different
bottles. Everything smelled so good. But it
was the perfume that had given her away each
time.

Robin peered into the mirror. Not too bad,
she thought. She used makeup base to cover
some of the bruises. Her hair was a mess,
though. It felt as if it was full of sand and dirt.

At two o'clock, a young nurse came in with a
wheelchair. "Well, don't we look nice," the
nurse said. "I'm Judy. Dr. Webber said you
wanted to visit your friend. Are you feeling up
to it?"

"Oh, yes." Robin started to scramble out of

bed and nearly fell. "Guess I'm weaker than I thought."

"Here, let me help you," Judy said.

The nurse helped Robin into the apple green robe, then she wheeled her out of the room. Robin looked around. She'd never been in a hospital before—except when she was born. Each section of the building had a nurses' station in the middle. A dozen pie-shaped rooms radiated out from the station. The nurses were only a few steps from any room.

"This is ICU just ahead," Judy said.

The intensive care unit was on the other side of the hospital. As they came to Shane's room, Robin whispered, "Wait!"

Judy leaned down. "Are you all right?"

"I—I'm scared."

"We can go back to your room if it's too upsetting."

"No. I have to see him."

Judy turned Robin over to an ICU nurse who was wearing cranberry-colored pants and a short-sleeved shirt instead of a white uniform.

"Remember, Robin," the nurse told her, "don't say anything negative in front of him. We don't know how much a person hears when he's in a coma. Talk to him. The doctor thinks it might help. His parents aren't able to be with him except at night."

"I know. His mom and dad both work even longer hours than my parents."

Robin took a deep, quivering breath. She was afraid she might cry or break down in front of Shane. "I guess I'm ready now."

But she wasn't really prepared. Behind and beside his bed was a confusing array of machines and tubes and bags and bottles all connected to Shane. He didn't even look like himself. A tube ran from his mouth to a machine beside the bed. Wires led from his chest to a smaller TV-like machine with little green lines running across the face of it. He was a mass of bruises and bandages. She had expected him to be absolutely still, but he was thrashing about as if in pain.

"Can't you give him anything?" Robin cried. "Can't you see he's hurting?"

"We don't know whether he feels the pain or not. But remember what I said—no negative remarks."

"What are those machines for?" Robin whispered.

"The large one is called a ventilator. It regulates his breathing. The other one with the green blips is a cardiac monitor that shows us his heart beat."

The ICU nurse wheeled Robin close to the

bed. "I'll be here in fifteen minutes to take you back to your room."

"Fifteen minutes? Is that all the time I get?"

"Yes. Shane needs rest and quiet. But during visitation hours you can come in once an hour," she said and left the room.

Robin could hardly bear to look at him. *Oh, Shane, you have to get well. It should have been me, not you. Please, I couldn't bear it if . . .*

She swallowed hard and tried to smile. "Shane? It's Robin. You're going to be—just fine. Before you know it, you'll have me running five miles every morn—" Her voice broke, and she couldn't go on.

She bowed her head. *Please, God, he's too young to die. I'll do anything—just make him be all right. . . .*

Three

DURING visiting hours that same evening, Shane's parents came into Robin's room while her mom and dad were there.

Robin could tell by Mrs. McAllister's red eyes that she had been crying. Shane's dad looked tired, and his face was drawn with worry.

"I had to leave his room," Mrs. McAllister said in a choked voice. "They told me not to show my feelings in front of Shane. How can I do that? It's killing me to see him lying there so helpless."

Robin's dad brought chairs for them. "Margaret, Sam, I can't tell you how sorry we are . . . ."

Mr. McAllister stalked around the room. His fists were jammed into his pockets. "I tell you, George, if I ever get my hands on that Haliburton kid, I'll—" He let the words hang there. "He'll probably get a slap on the wrist and be out on the street again to hurt some other child."

Robin's mother had her arm around Mrs. McAllister. "Maybe not. They've been cracking down harder on drunk drivers."

"He's a kid," Mr. McAllister said harshly. "And his folks have money. They'll get him off. But he's not going to get away with it. If Shane isn't better in a few days, I'm suing."

"Sam, please," Mrs. McAllister said. "This isn't the time to talk about money."

"It's not the money! That boy has to learn a lesson."

Nobody said anything for a moment, then Mrs. McAllister turned to Robin.

"Robin? Are you all right? I've been so upset over Shane, I'm afraid I haven't been very thoughtful. Your little face is so bruised— is it painful?"

"I'm okay. Shane pushed me out of the way . . ." Robin closed her eyes, unable to go on. *It should have been me.*

"If all Robin's tests show no problems," her mother broke in, "she should be able to come home tomorrow or the next day."

"I really appreciate your sitting with Shane when we're not here, Robin." Mrs. McAllister stood up and gave a tired sigh. "I'd hate for him to wake up and be all alone." Her voice broke again. "Sam, we'd better be going. I want to go back and tell Shane good night."

"If there's anything—anything at all we can do, please let us know," Robin's mother said.

"Thanks." The McAllisters started to leave, then Shane's mother turned around. "Oh, I almost forgot. The hospital gave us a sack of things. Some of them may be yours, Robin. I can't bear to look in it yet. Would you like to— to go through it?"

"Maybe you should wait until you're home," Robin's mother said.

"No, please, I'd like to see it. Shane won a stuffed animal and a hat for me. Maybe they're there. I was afraid . . ."

"I'll get the sack," Mr. McAllister told her. "I'll leave it on our way out."

* * * * *

Robin waited until her parents left before she opened the blue plastic bag sitting beside her on the bed. *Please let the rabbit and hat be there.*

She held the large crinkly bag in her lap for a long time before she could look inside.

There were the crazy toys and jewelry they'd won. She spotted the green feather, pulled it out, and stroked it against her cheek. He'd said it matched her eyes. She dug in the sack and found the pink hat. It was crushed and muddy. *Oh, Shane, I was so stupid. It's a beautiful hat.* As she stuck the feather into the band and put the hat on her head, tears streamed down her face.

Hardly able to see, she dumped out the rest of the things in the bag. The rabbit tumbled onto the bed. One ear was gone, and his white fur was stained and grimy. Robin held the stuffed rabbit close and whispered, "I'll never let you out of my sight."

Carefully she took off the hat and placed it on the bedside table. When the nurse came in to get her ready for night, she was still cradling the rabbit and singing softly, "Old MacDonald had a farm. Ee—ay—ee—ay—oh. . . ."

* * * * *

The next afternoon, the nurse named Judy came in again. She removed the IV tube from Robin's hand, then she helped Robin into her robe. As Judy wheeled her to Shane's room, she reminded Robin, "Talk to him naturally, just as if he were conscious."

Robin moved the wheelchair close to the bed. Shane was lying in a different position.

His color was bad, and there were dark circles under his eyes. He lay quietly. The heart monitor traced its green line across the screen. The ventilator made its swish-swish sound. In a nearby room, someone was moaning.

Robin put the pink hat on her head and set the rabbit on her knee. Forcing herself to sound happy and natural, she smiled and said, "Hey, Shane, look, I'm wearing the hat." Her voice sounded too shrill even to her own ears.

She could see no flicker of response in his face. Oh, why did we have that dumb argument? she thought. Maybe he's still angry with me.

"Shane? I brought the rabbit. I'll have to take him home and clean him up a bit, but he's okay. We'll have to think of a name for him, though. We can't go around calling him Rabbit." She laid the stuffed animal on the bed beside him. "The two of us will come every day to see you. But you'd better hurry up and get out of here. I don't want to go jogging alone. Remember that morning when we came around the corner of the post office and the cop who was driving by thought we had done something wrong?" She tried to laugh, but it sounded more like a cry. "I thought for sure he was going to haul us in . . . ."

Shane's eyes remained closed. His face was still expressionless. She leaned close. "Shane,

41

why can't you hear me?" she whispered.

At the sound of the ICU nurse coming into the room, Robin turned. "He doesn't even know I'm here," she said, trying to hold back tears.

"We don't know if he can hear you. Talk to him about a fun time you had together. Just don't get discouraged."

Robin nodded. "Is it all right if—if I touch him—hold his hand?"

"Yes, but don't tire yourself out, honey."

Feeling self-conscious, Robin took Shane's hand in her own. As soon as the nurse left, Robin said softly, "Remember the first time we went skiing? I felt so stupid when I took off down the wrong hill and landed against the tree—one leg on each side! If it hadn't been for you, I might not have ever tried again."

Robin traced little circles on Shane's hand. "I think that was the most fun I've had in my entire life. Well, almost—except for the first time you kissed me."

She gently squeezed his hand. "Shane, remember that lodge that overlooked the lake? The water was so blue, and all around it were those snow-covered mountains. I loved the way the icicles hung from all the windows—and the big stone fireplace and how we danced. . . ."

Robin closed her eyes. That evening they had discovered they both loved hot chocolate and even hotter chili and reruns of *Happy Days* and art and old horror movies and popcorn dripping with melted butter. They'd even found they hated the same things—too much homework, adults who ask you questions, then don't listen to your answers, blisters on your heels, soggy pizzas, dogs that try to bite when you're out jogging. Tears welled to her eyes. Would Shane ever run again—ever catch another pass?

She gently released his hand, pushed away from the bed, and buried her face in her arms so he couldn't hear her cry—if he could hear anything. . . .

"Robin?"

She looked up to see Judy with the wheelchair. Robin scrubbed at her eyes.

"I'm sorry to bother you, but you have company in your room."

"My mom and dad?"

"No. Two girls about your age."

Robin didn't really want to talk to anybody, but she guessed she should see who had come to visit her. She looked at Shane. "I'll come back tomorrow. I'll bring my cassette player so we can listen to some of your favorite tapes." She got the rabbit from the bed, then realized

43

she was still wearing the hat. "Shane won these for me," she said defensively. "He likes me to wear the hat."

"It's cute," Judy said as she rolled Robin out of the room. "The feather matches your eyes."

Robin burst into tears.

Several visitors looked the other way and hurried by.

The nurse pushed the chair to a quiet corner. "Go ahead and cry."

Robin kept shaking her head. "It's so dumb. I—almost the last thing Shane said to me was about the feather."

"I'm sorry. Would you rather not see your friends? I can tell them you're not up to having visitors."

"No, I'm all right. They'll want to know about Shane."

Judy handed Robin a tissue and started the chair rolling again.

"Do you need help getting back into bed?" Judy asked when they reached Robin's room.

"No, I feel fine. And thanks for coming to get me."

Robin squared her shoulders and took a deep breath before pushing herself into the room.

Jackie and Cheryl were fiddling with the

remote control for the TV. Robin was glad to see them. The three of them always did everything together. Over the years they had all wanted to be ballerinas, nurses, artists, and ski instructors. This year they'd all decided to be lawyers.

Robin overheard Jackie say, "Do you think Shane will be like those cases on the news? You know, live for years like a vegetable?"

"Don't even think such an awful thing!" Robin cried. "He's going to be out of here—soon."

"Hey, Robin, I'm sorry," Jackie said. "Wow, you look like you were in a fight."

Still a little angry, Robin answered coolly, "I was lucky."

"How is Shane?" Cheryl asked. "Have you seen him?"

"I was just in his room, but he can't have regular visitors yet."

Suddenly tired, Robin climbed onto the bed and leaned back against the pillows. She held the rabbit close. "Thanks for coming to see me. But I should be back to school next week."

"Hey, Robin, did you see last night's newspaper?" Cheryl asked.

"No, Mom forgot to bring one, I guess."

"We brought a copy." Cheryl dug into her

red school bag. "You made the front page." She handed Robin the Woodbridge Sentinel.

"I think they should have had your picture," Jackie said.

Robin gave a strained laugh. "Not with these bruises."

She spread the paper on her lap. *TWO WOODBRIDGE TEENAGERS INJURED IN CRASH.*

Fifteen-year-old Shane McAllister and fourteen-year-old Robin Nichols were injured Friday evening in a freak accident.

The '82 Oldsmobile, driven by Troy Haliburton, eighteen, spun out of control on the slippery street. The car ran up over the curb and smashed into a bus stop bench, striking the two young people.

The accident occurred on Broadway and . . .

Robin wadded up the paper. "They make it sound like it wasn't Troy's fault at all!" she said angrily. "Freak accident, my foot. He was drunk!"

"It doesn't even mention that in the story," Jackie said. "Bet his parents paid somebody off."

What will Pat Erickson think about this? Robin wondered. "There was a radio reporter here this morning. She won't leave anything out of her story."

"Wow, you're getting famous here," Jackie said. "Pretty soon, you won't even speak to us."

"I'd rather find a better way to get my name in the paper than by being in an accident," Robin said and tossed the paper aside. "The radio reporter was talking about a student group. Have you two ever heard of SADD?"

"I saw a movie on TV about how it got started," Cheryl said. "It was good. Hey, Robin, guess what. Mrs. Hansen has been out with the flu," Cheryl went on. "The sub put five guys on detention yesterday. Jeri Williams broke a tooth in gym. Sheila and Maria were kicked out of Home Ec—just because they set fire to the kitchen. And Milo Anderson got suspended."

"No kidding," Robin said, but she knew her voice sounded flat. Cheryl and Jackie giggled and talked back and forth about school. Robin wanted to join in, but now all the school stuff seemed dumb and unimportant.

She broke in. "Have you heard anything about Troy Haliburton? Is he back in school?"

"Yeah. We heard he lost his driver's license. Boy, was he a real jerk."

"They probably won't do anything to him," Robin said, resentfully. "I'll bet he doesn't even come to the hospital."

47

"I don't think I would," Cheryl said. "I'd be too ashamed."

"Hey, let's talk about something else," Jackie said. "We came to cheer you up." She dug into a bag. "Here are a couple of magazines."

"Thanks," Robin said, taking them and putting them on the bed. "It gets pretty boring in here."

Nobody said anything for a bit, and Robin realized they were ill at ease. Finally Jackie glanced at her watch and said brightly, "I didn't know it was so late. We hate to rush, Robin, but I promised to help Mom."

"Me, too," Cheryl said. "I have a ton of homework and . . ." Her voice trailed off. "We'll try to get back again, though."

"I'll be home by tomorrow. But thanks for coming—and for the magazines. I really appreciate it," Robin said.

Yet, as she watched the two girls leave, Robin couldn't help feeling almost relieved. Jackie was far from the most tactful person in the world. And their obvious unease made Robin feel uncomfortable, too. She thought about what she'd overheard Jackie saying.

Shane a vegetable? No way.

Four

THE next afternoon, Robin's father was taking time off work to bring her home from the hospital. Before he was due to arrive, she asked if she could go in to see Shane. Even though it wasn't visiting hours, the head nurse gave her permission.

She dressed and packed her things, all but the hat and rabbit, then walked to ICU. She pulled a chair up close to the bed and looked at Shane for a few moments. There seemed to be no change that she could see. She put the hat on at a cocky angle and snapped the elastic under her chin.

Reaching for his hand, she held it to her cheek and spoke softly. "I'm going home now, Shane, but I'll come to see you every day after school . . . . I wish you'd open your eyes so you could see I'm wearing my hat."

His hand twitched slightly. She held her

breath. It jerked again, stronger this time. "Shane? Can you hear me?" she asked excitedly. "It's Robin. If you can hear me, squeeze my hand again. Shane, open your eyes!" she cried. "You can do it!"

The nurse came hurrying in. "What is it, Robin? What's wrong?"

"He's coming out of the coma. He squeezed my hand. See! Don't you see?"

"I'm sorry, dear, it's just muscle spasms. Sometimes he gets them in his legs, too."

"But look, he's making a face. He's trying to smile. He's going to be all right!"

The nurse took Robin by the arm and drew her away from the bed. She shook her head. "He's just grimacing. It means nothing."

"No!" Robin cried. "You're wrong. He's going to wake up any minute now."

"Come on back to your room. You're much too upset."

Robin pulled away and returned to Shane's side. "I have to be here in case he wakes up. His mother doesn't want him to wake up and be all alone."

"It's not good for the patient when you get excited. Anyway, the nurses' station is only a few feet away. He's being monitored. We'll know."

Robin looked at the nurse, then at Shane.

"You're sure?"

"I'm sure," the nurse said softly.

Robin touched Shane's hand and whispered, "I'll be back tomorrow, Shane. I promise."

* * * * *

"Well, here we are—home again," Robin's father said as he opened the car door and started to lift Robin out.

"Daddy, I can walk."

"Humor me," he said. He picked her up in his arms and shut the car door with his leg. "I used to do this when you were a baby."

"I feel kind of dumb now, though."

He paused on the porch steps and looked down at Robin, as if he were memorizing her face. "Honey," he said softly, "do you have any idea how we felt when we got a call from the hospital?"

"I guess I do."

His face twisted. "That ride in the rain was terrible. We thought—" Robin saw him blink back tears. "We thought we'd lost you."

Then he squeezed her and gave her a forced grin. "But we have you safe now, so let me baby you just a little."

She had to admit it felt good to be at home, to feel safe and loved.

He carried her into the house and to the living room couch. "How about some ice cream? I bought your favorite—chocolate and peanut butter crunch."

"Sounds good. All I ever got in the hospital was vanilla."

While her dad was in the kitchen, Robin picked up the newspaper on the coffee table and reread the article about the accident. It still made her angry. Troy had been charged with drunk driving, so why wasn't it mentioned in the paper?

Her father returned with a tray and a huge dish of ice cream. "I see you've read the story."

"Dad, do you think they'll do anything to Troy?"

"I don't know. Sam McAllister is going to bring a civil suit. But that won't punish Troy, only his folks."

Robin's dad noticed she wasn't eating. "Come on, honey, eat up before that ice cream melts."

"Remember when we used to come home late?" Robin asked. "You'd carry me to my room, then bring me a dish of ice cream. I'd wake up later with my face practically in the melted ice cream."

"I remember. The last couple of days I've

52

been remembering a lot of things. I'm sure not going to take life for granted anymore."

"Me neither," Robin said. "When everything started to go black after the crash, I thought I was going to die."

"Well, thank God, you're all right. Your mom and I did some heavy praying, I'll tell you." He gave her a quick hug. "I hate to leave you alone, but I have to get some work done. I'll be in the study if you need anything."

"I think I'll go to my room after I finish my ice cream. I guess I'm still tired."

He kissed the top of her head. "You call me if you need anything. Mom promised to get home early, but maybe we'll surprise her, and I'll order a pizza with everything on it."

"I didn't get that in the hospital, either."

As she took little bites of ice cream, letting it melt on her tongue, she looked around the familiar living room. She had only been in the hospital for three days, but she was seeing the house with new eyes. After the sterile hospital room, her home looked so comfortable. She liked the gleaming maple furniture, all the pictures, the little figurines, and the tiny brass and pewter pots filled with plants. Uncle Burt called them "dust-catchers."

She finished every drop of the ice cream, then carried the dish to the kitchen and rinsed it off. She ran her fingers over the dishwasher. Shane had touched it just the other day. . . .

Robin hurried to her room and flung herself on the bed. Why did the accident have to happen? Why did Troy have to drive by while they were waiting for the bus? Why had the buses been full? Why was Shane lying helpless in a hospital bed? A million questions whirled around in her head, but there were no answers.

She got out the pink hat and rabbit and tried to clean the spots. When she finished she set the rabbit on a shelf and hung the hat on a hook on the wall. As she was standing there, she caught a glimpse of some red writing on her dresser mirror. For a second she was angry. Who would write on her mirror with lipstick?

She moved closer so she could read the words. I LOVE YOU, ROBIN.

"Shane," she breathed softly. "Oh, Shane. . . ."

He must have written it when he came in here to get my coat, she thought. With tears running down her face, she outlined the letters with her fingers. She knew that Shane loved her, but he'd never spoken those words to her.

She heard the front door chimes, then heard her father open the door.

"Hello, Cheryl, Jackie. Come on in. I think

Robin's in her room. I'll see if she's awake."

Robin quickly threw a scarf over the mirror. The words were too private to share with anyone else. She hurriedly climbed into bed and pretended to be asleep. Right now, she couldn't talk to anyone.

Shane was coming home soon. And he had written, I LOVE YOU, ROBIN.

Five

ROBIN sank into a fitful sleep. . . . *Rain glistened on the slippery street. The car's headlights pierced her brain. The silent scream of the driver echoed her own. Shane!*

She awakened to find her pillow damp and knew she had been crying in her dream. Unable to sleep, she crossed to the window. Streaks of red and pink mottled the pre-dawn sky. That was a sure sign of a storm, Uncle Burt used to say.

Shivering in the cold room, she slipped into her gray sweats. She really didn't feel like jogging, but Shane always claimed that it cleared the brain and made you forget all your problems. As she pulled on her two pair of cotton socks and running shoes, she sighed. I hope Shane is right, she thought, because Mom and Dad are going to kill me for going out jogging after just being in the hospital.

She slipped quietly out the front door. When she started down the sidewalk to the park where she and Shane ran on weekends, she realized she was weaker than she had expected. She settled for a fast walk.

As she followed their regular route, memories flooded back. She passed the spot where the dog had bitten her ankle. She remembered the exact place where Shane had talked about his hopes of getting a football scholarship to Stanford or USC. She passed the maple tree where he had asked her to go to a movie—an awful, horror movie. In a scary scene she had jumped and knocked the popcorn out of his hand. They had both leaned down to catch the box and had bumped heads. And he had kissed the sore spot on her forehead.

It had been the spring of last year when she had gone jogging with him for the first time. He had goaded her into getting up at the ridiculous hour of six o'clock. She would have much rather slept in on a cool Saturday morning, but she had dragged herself out of bed and met him on the front porch.

He was bouncing up and down on his toes and doing stretching exercises; she was yawning and rubbing her gritty eyes.

"Good morning," he said cheerfully.

"What's so good about it?" she grumbled.

"You're alive. You're healthy. The birds are singing. You're—"

"I'm sleepy. And I hate people who are cheerful in the mornings. It's against nature."

He grinned. "Stop griping, Birdie, and start your stretching exercises."

She forced a scowl. It was hard to pretend to be unhappy around Shane. "Why did I let you talk me into this?" Stifling another yawn, she did as he told her. When she was warmed up, they started off at a brisk walk.

"You have to start out slowly, or you'll get shin splints and sore muscles," he told her. "But after you run for a few weeks, you'll feel good and have so much energy that you'll never want to sleep in again."

"Sure," she said doubtfully.

They headed for Woodbridge Park and jogged on the oak-lined trails along the lake.

When Shane let her stop and rest for a few minutes, she watched the pale yellow sun rise over the mountains to the east. Her breath smoked in the splintery air. She stretched her arms as if she could reach the sun.

"I hate to say it, Shane, but this is a great time of day."

He gave her an I-told-you-so grin and started off again.

That first week or so, she hadn't been able to talk and run, but as she grew stronger and her chest didn't feel as if it were on fire, they talked about wanting to travel to other places, other countries.

"I'd like to go to the Olympics some day. Even if I don't compete, I'd like to be there."

"That would be fun," she agreed, "but I want to go to the Greek Isles and sail on a yacht and go diving for sunken treasure."

"And go skiing in the Alps."

"And walk to the bottom of the Grand Canyon. Oh, Shane, there are so many things to do. It'll take us years . . . ."

Now, she sank down on a bench and wondered if they would ever do any of those things. Shane was missing the football season. It wasn't fair. Troy would probably get his scholarship while Shane lay in a coma. Well, he's going to get better. I'll help him get back in shape, she thought.

She jumped up, took off at a run, and didn't slow down until she reached home.

* * * * *

Robin dreaded going back to school. There would be so many questions. She straightened her shoulders. There will be just as many questions tomorrow, she thought. Robin headed across the campus and had only walked a short distance when a group of kids gathered around her.

"Hey, Robin, how're you doing?"

"You look great—except for the bruises."

"Boy, I guess you and Shane were really lucky."

Robin looked from one to another, unable to get a word in.

"Is he still in intensive care?"

"We heard he's in a coma. Is that right?"

"Have you heard about Troy?"

Robin cringed under the onslaught of questions. "I'm fine. Shane's in a coma, but I'm sure he'll be back in school in a couple of weeks. What about Troy?"

"He got kicked off the football team," a boy said. "I think that's crummy. It's not like he's on drugs or anything."

Robin began to shake, partly from anger, partly from stress. She tried to close out the voices but they went on and on.

"Yeah, without Shane and Troy, we'll probably lose all the rest of our games."

"Well, I think they should kick Troy out of school."

"Are you and Shane's parents going to sue the Haliburtons? Bet you could get a million, especially if Shane doesn't come out of the coma."

The trembling grew worse. *Leave me alone! Leave me alone!*

Cheryl came up then and took Robin's arm. "Hey, guys, give her a break. Can't you see she's upset?"

Cheryl led Robin to the girls' restroom and watched quietly while Robin splashed her face with cool water.

Robin took a deep breath. "How do people go through press conferences? All those questions make you feel like you're on trial."

"It burns me up how some of the kids take Troy's side," Cheryl said angrily.

Robin was thinking about the organization the reporter had mentioned. "I'm beginning to think we do need a SADD chapter here. Maybe the kids would get some sense."

"You know, you're probably right, Robin. Another kid who was drinking with Troy that night put a dent in his parents' car. He's grounded."

"He's lucky. He could be like Shane."

As they walked to their homeroom, Cheryl filled Robin in on what had happened the last couple of days.

"Saturday, a bunch of us are going on an all-day ride to Lake Morris. Are you still too sore to ride your bike?"

"I feel fine now, but I don't want to miss my afternoon visit to the hospital. I only get fifteen minutes at a time."

Cheryl nodded. "Okay. But it won't be as much fun without you two." Cheryl giggled. "Remember when we all went to the circus and Shane dressed up like a clown?"

"Yeah, he got into the ring with the other clowns, and nobody even realized it until the ringmaster noticed he had one too many clowns."

They both laughed.

"Tell him the gang will be up to see him as soon as he can have visitors," Cheryl said. "Mike and Bob went up last night, but they weren't allowed in."

"I know. He needs his rest until he comes out of the coma."

Cheryl stopped and nudged Robin's arm. "Guess who's coming toward us!"

Robin looked up to see Troy walking slowly down the path. He was reading some papers and hadn't seen them yet. Panic and anger filled Robin. "I don't want to talk to him—not now, not here," she whispered.

"It's too late. He's seen us."

There wasn't room for Troy to pass. They stopped. Troy stopped. His face was pale, and he avoided their eyes. Then without a word he cut across the grass.

Robin turned to watch him hurry away. Her hand clenched into a fist. If it hadn't been for him, Shane wouldn't be lying in a hospital bed, she thought.

"Do you think Troy has tried to see Shane?" Cheryl asked.

"I don't think so." Robin's jaw tensed with anger. "He's never even called me. You'd think he'd have the decency to ask if I'm okay. Cheryl, I've made up my mind. I'm going to call that radio reporter and get her to help us set up a SADD chapter. Let's meet at my place Saturday night and talk about it."

"I'll tell the kids, but I don't know if anyone has the time."

"It only takes an instant for a drunk driver to hit someone, but we don't have time to do anything about it?" Robin's voice rose. "If you guys won't help, I'll find someone who will!"

"Hey, don't get upset," Cheryl said quickly. "We'll be there Saturday."

The bell rang, and they hurried into their homeroom. Again, Robin had to answer a lot of questions. But she made it through the day without too much trouble until her last class.

Hoping to avoid talking to anyone, she got to the art room before any of the other kids.

The room was light and cheerful, with lots of windows. Sketches, oil paintings, and water colors from the more advanced classes hung on every available wall space. She loved the smell of paint and turpentine. Art was the only class that she and Shane were in together. It was her favorite class, and Mr. Matheson was her favorite teacher. He was busy at an easel and didn't notice Robin step inside the door.

The first thing she saw was Shane's work table and stool.

She stood there frozen. Kids pushed past her, but she was barely aware of them.

"Robin?"

She could almost see Shane perched on the round stool, his head bent over his drawing board, and laughing at his own cartoon. She tried to walk over to her table next to his, but her feet wouldn't move.

"Robin? Are you all right?"

She felt a hand on her shoulder and looked up to see Mr. Matheson. "What? I'm sorry, I—"

"I said, are you all right? You're white as chalk. Are you sick?"

"Yes," she answered quickly. "May I be excused from class?"

"Of course. I'll give you a pass. Take it to the office."

She knew she was being silly. But seeing

that empty stool hurt too much.

* * * * *

Robin rested in the nurse's room until school was out, then headed for the bus stop. She tried to push down the dread of seeing that corner again. Luckily, the day was cold and sunny, not at all like the evening of the accident. She waited for the bus with a group of other kids. Every time a car pulled close to the curb, fear shot through her, and her heart raced. She kept hearing the skid of tires, the awful sound of grinding metal, her own scream.

All right, Robin, get a hold of yourself. It's just like getting back on a horse or a bicycle after a fall. Your nerves are shot, that's all.

Once she was settled on the bus, she relaxed a little and tried to think of some funny things to tell Shane. She kept looking at her watch, not wanting to miss any of the precious time with him. The trip only took fifteen minutes, but it seemed like hours before the bus stopped in front of Woodbridge General.

She got off the bus and hurried up to ICU. At the desk she asked if it would be all right to go in to see Shane. "Is he any better today?"

"There's no change," the nurse told her. "It takes time."

"I've brought him some of his favorite tapes. Is it okay to play them?"

"It's an excellent idea," the nurse said. "You can go in now."

Robin stopped in the doorway and looked at Shane. His condition seemed to be the same, except that he was more agitated. He was thrashing his head back and forth on the pillow. Now he had a small tube in his nose that was connected to a bag of milky liquid. She was afraid he might pull loose from all the tubes.

She pulled a chair up close to the bed and opened her pack. She put on the pink hat and sat Rabbit on the bed. "I couldn't get all the mud off," she said, "but at least he's cleaner now. I've decided to call him Rabbit, unless you've come up with a better name."

She dug out the recorder. "Shane? I have a surprise for you. I brought the two tapes you gave me on my birthday. The nurse said it was okay. I'm sure glad you don't have some old guy in here with you who hates rock music."

Placing a tape in the player, she turned it on low. She took Shane's hand, and after a while he seemed calmer.

"Shane? I went jogging this morning—well,

walking anyhow. It's not the same without you, though. I need you to spur me on.

"I went back to school today, too. Everybody asked about you. As soon as you're out of intensive care, you'll have a lot of company."

She kept talking, although it was hard to keep up a one-sided conversation. "I had to make up a test I missed. I'll bet I get a *D* on it. I just couldn't seem to think today." She frowned. That sounded too negative. She forced a smile. "The kids are all going to Morris Lake Saturday. I'll bet by then you'll be able to go.

"And Saturday evening we're getting together to talk about organizing a group against drunk driving. You can be our first speaker. And you can draw the pictures for flyers and stuff and we—we . . ."

She suddenly felt stupid and miserable talking on and on with no reply from Shane. She leaned forward and searched his face for any response.

"Shane, I know you can hear me. I just know it. I—I found your note on the mirror. Did you really mean it? Or were you just being funny?"

If he would just squeeze my hand, she thought. If he could give me some sign, any- thing. "Please tell me, Shane. Please?"

Six

"BEFORE we start," Robin said, "does anyone want something to drink? I have cola, root beer, orange, or cider."

When everyone was settled, Robin took her own drink and sat on the arm of the big chair. Bob and Mike leaned against the wall, looking as if they wanted to leave. Cheryl and Jackie were on the couch, and Pat Erickson, the reporter, was sitting cross-legged on the floor.

In jeans and a red sweater, Pat looked younger than she had at the hospital. She opened her briefcase and pulled out a bunch of papers and brochures. "I was really glad to get your call, Robin. I've had this material for SADD for some time, but it takes you students to get a chapter started. It has to be your problem, your challenge, your need to do something constructive."

"But we don't have any idea how to start,"

Robin said.

"I don't know if I want to start anything," Bob said. "What good can we do? None of us drink."

"Well, let me tell you some of the 'sad facts,'" Pat said. "Injury from alcohol-caused crashes is the number one health problem for teenagers. You might not drink, but you ride in cars with your friends. Teenage passengers show a high death rate starting at age 13. Someone is killed by a drunk driver every twenty-three minutes."

Robin looked around the room. She could tell they were all stunned by the statistics.

"So how could this SADD thing have kept Shane and Robin from getting hurt?" Mike asked belligerently, as if he didn't want to believe what Pat had told him.

"Maybe one of Troy's friends would have said, 'Hey, man, you've had too much to drink. You'd better not drive. Call your parents. Take a taxi. But don't get behind that wheel.'"

"Oh, sure," Bob said sarcastically. "Nobody listens when he's having a good time."

"Right," Jackie said. "They'd tell us to mind our own business."

"Give her a chance," Robin said. "Do you want more of us to end up in the hospital—like Shane?"

"Look," Pat said, "I know what peer pressure is. You kids have to realize that it's okay to say no to a drink, or no to a ride with someone who's been drinking. A peer counseling program is part of SADD's objectives."

"So how do we get started?" Robin asked. "I'll bet we'd have to get permission from a hundred people."

"You have to meet with the student council and talk to the principal and to the school administration to get their cooperation. Then you need to choose a faculty advisor and select officers."

"Coach Adams would make a great faculty advisor," Robin said. "He thinks a lot of Shane."

"You'll need an honorary chairperson—like the mayor or a sports personality," Pat went on.

"How about you, Pat?" Robin asked, and looked around at the others. "Don't you think Pat should be our honorary chairperson?"

Everyone nodded.

"Then what do we do?" Robin asked.

"Organize a SADD DAY, and set up your activities for the year."

Jackie was shaking her head. "This is getting complicated. We'd never have time for it."

"A lot of activities are fun—like placing a wrecked car in front of your school as a SADD reminder. Smashing a junker for SADD—five whacks with a sledgehammer for a buck—is a good way to raise money. That money can buy bumper stickers and SADD T-shirts. You can write a skit. I'll see that it gets on the radio station."

"I still think it'll take too much time," Jackie said.

Robin jumped up. This was something they could do. This was something for Shane. "So we get other people to help," she said, her voice filled with excitement. "I'll talk to the class presidents, the Pep Club, all the different school clubs, the Booster Club, and the PTA."

"Hey, maybe we could do a music video," Mike said, beginning to warm up to the idea.

"Or a walk-a-thon," Cheryl put in.

"One idea from SADD is to challenge your principal to spend a night in jail if 95 percent of the students join SADD," Pat told them.

"I'll go for that one," Bob said. "Only I'd rather it be old Ledbetter."

"Well, what do you all think?" Robin asked.

"I guess we could try," Mike said.

"I'm in," Bob told them.

Cheryl sighed. "Me, too."

Jackie nodded reluctantly.

Pat gave them some more pointers on how to get the chapter started, then she got to her feet. "It will make a difference. I promise you it will."

* * * * *

In the activity room, Robin stretched out her legs and leaned back. "I'm beat," she told Pat. "I can't believe we accomplished so much in just three weeks."

"You've done a terrific job, Robin. And I thought you said you didn't have any organizational ability." Pat grinned. "I'll be your press agent when you run for president."

Robin turned and smiled back. "I sure couldn't have done it without you. But I'm scared. What if hardly anyone shows up today?"

At this first meeting, they had invited Coach Adams as faculty advisor, the presidents of each class, and a representative from each of the school organizations.

Before Robin had time to get too nervous, Mike, Bob, Cheryl, and Jackie came in. Then everyone seemed to arrive at once.

Robin sat in the middle of a long table with Pat on one side. The other side was saved for the football coach. Robin was busy acknowledging the people taking their seats when she saw Coach Adams come in with Troy.

Anger boiled up and burned her insides as if she'd swallowed acid.

As she jumped up, her chair scraped the floor with a loud screech. She charged across the room to where Troy was standing alone by the door.

"What're you doing here?" she demanded. "How dare you show your face at a SADD meeting?"

He avoided her eyes. "Coach asked me to come," Troy said flatly.

"What're you trying to do—butter him up so you'll get back on the team?" Her voice rose but she didn't care.

"Robin," Pat called. "We need you."

Still shaking with anger, Robin took her place at the table. Her face felt hot. She took a deep breath, and tried to control her trembling voice.

"Hi, everybody. We really appreciate your coming. I guess you all know we're starting a chapter of SADD, Students Against Driving Drunk, in our school. And you know Shane McAllister is in the hospital in a coma because of a"—her throat tightened with anger, and she fixed her eyes on Troy, who was staring at the floor—"because of a drunk driver."

She felt Pat's hand cover hers and took another deep breath. "We think SADD can save some other kid from suffering the way Shane and his family have.

"To tell you more about the objectives, here is our honorary chairperson, Pat Erickson, from radio station WBY."

Pat stood up, and everyone clapped politely. "Thanks, Robin." She smiled, then moved out from behind the table and casually sat on the edge.

"I don't know how much you know about SADD. There are both high school and jr. high chapters. The organization was started by Robert Anastas, a coach. The deaths of two of his hockey players in drunk driving accidents drove him to organize SADD. He says there is too little communication between teenagers and parents. He absolutely does not condone underage drinking, but he's written up a 'Contract for Life.'" She held up a sheet of paper. "The student agrees to call the parent for advice and/or transportation if he's in a situation where he's been drinking or the person driving has been drinking. The parent agrees to come and pick up the student at any hour, no questions asked at that time."

"My dad would never sign that!" one boy

said. "He wouldn't ask questions, he'd just belt me one."

Others gave their objections.

"My mom wouldn't get out of bed to come and get me."

"My old man comes home drunk every Saturday night. I sure wouldn't want him coming to pick me up!"

"I don't want my mom and dad to know I've been at a party where there's drinking or drugs."

"Your concerns are all very valid. Part of the program," Pat told them, "is to get parents and the whole community to understand the problems and then get them involved in combatting drunk driving.

"Another important aspect of the program," Pat went on, "is to eliminate peer pressure to drink and to drive under the influence of drugs or alcohol."

Pat walked around the room as she continued telling some of the objectives of SADD. "We have to do something about the problem. More than 50,000 Americans died in the Vietnam War. Drinking drivers have killed more people than that in two years alone."

She gave them some of the statistics that she had told Robin's friends. Suddenly she whirled and pointed her finger at Mike. "Do you think people should drive who are drunk?"

Startled, Mike blurted out, "No!"

Pat turned to the president of the senior class. "Do you think drunks should drive?"

"Uh—well, heck no."

"Nobody thinks that," Pat said. "Nobody!"

She didn't say anything for a minute, just walked around the room, stopping in front of each person briefly. Then she spoke so softly that everybody leaned forward to hear.

"Then why do we let our friends get behind the wheel of a car when they've had too much to drink?"

She gave everybody a chance to give their opinions.

"How can you stop somebody when it's his own car?"

"What are you supposed to do—handcuff him?"

"Anyway, it's his business."

"How can you tell if somebody's really had too much?"

Pat moved to the front of the room again. "A few years ago, I was faced with that problem. And I asked the same questions. My boyfriend and I had been to a party to celebrate our coming marriage. Neither of us were really drinkers, but our hosts served champagne. It's rude to say, no, isn't it?"

76

Pat gave a harsh laugh. "I wish to God I had said no. That was my first mistake of the night."

"We had a wonderful time—were feeling no pain, as they say. When it was time to leave, my fiance—his name was Greg—stumbled a little on the way to the car. I said, 'Greg, honey, let's call a cab.'

" 'Why a cab?' " he asked. 'I feel fine. I've never felt better in my life.' He kissed me and helped me into the car.

"That was my second big mistake."

She bowed her head for a moment. There wasn't a sound in the room. When she raised her head, tears sparkled in her eyes. Her voice was flat and emotionless. "We hit a telephone pole. Greg was—killed instantly."

"I lived," she said almost in a whisper. "And I could have prevented his death. I have to live with that for the rest of my life."

She gave a long sigh and stood up straight. "It's up to all of you. Isn't it worth the time and effort if we can keep just one of our friends from being hurt or killed. The SADD slogan is, If we can dream it—it can be done. So, let's do it!"

As Pat sat down, the clapping was enthusiastic this time. Robin leaned over and whispered, "You were wonderful."

The other kids gathered around, all talking at once.

"Count me in."

"I'll do what I can."

"My brother's in Jr. High. Maybe he can get a SADD chapter started there, too."

"I'll bet we can get every kid in school to join."

Robin winked at her friends. "We did it. We're off and running."

Seven

ROBIN'S breath came in great gasps as she tried to keep up with Shane. The day was hot, and sweat dripped down her forehead and neck. Shane was a few yards ahead when she heard the roar of a powerful engine. She turned to look back over her shoulder and saw a black car like a hearse bearing down on them.

Shane! she screamed.

He could easily have outdistanced the car, but he stopped to wait for her. The car kept coming closer and closer. And now she could see that no one was behind the wheel.

The evil black car shot forward. She screamed. The car lights burned into her brain.

"Robin! Wake up!"

The overhead light blinded her for a minute, and she covered her eyes with her arms.

"Robin! What's wrong?" Her mother sat on the edge of the bed and pulled Robin's arms away from her face. "Honey, it's all right, it's all right."

Robin felt her mother's comforting arms, but she couldn't stop shaking. "I had a terrible dream. It was so real, so awful."

Her mother pulled the covers up around Robin's shoulders and adjusted the pillow. "Robin, we're worried about you. You can't let the accident affect your life forever."

"I'll be okay once Shane's out of the coma and back home. Oh, Mom when I saw him today he was so thin, and his skin was all withered. They're feeding him high protein food through a tube, but he's losing more weight all the time."

Her mother was quiet for a while. "Honey," she said finally, "I know you like to visit him, but I don't think you should go every day. You're tired all the time. Visiting Shane and keeping up with your school work and all this work you're doing for SADD—it's making you sick. Just because they elected you president doesn't mean you have to do everything yourself."

"Mom, I have a bad dream, and you make a big deal out of it."

Her mother sighed. "I just want you to promise to get more rest. Have a little fun and relax."

"How can I have fun while Shane is . . ." Her throat choked up, and she couldn't go on.

"I know SADD is important to you and Shane is important to you, but you're only fourteen. You need to get on with your life."

No one really understands, Robin thought.

"Mom, I know I'm helping him. Sometimes, I'm sure he can hear me." She sat up in bed and said eagerly, "The nurse says he's better. He might even move out of intensive care pretty soon."

"That's wonderful, honey."

"Just let me keep seeing him every day, and I promise I'll get more rest."

"All right." Her mother shivered in the cold room. "Now, how about a glass of milk and a cookie to help you get back to sleep?"

Robin's eyes were already getting heavy. "I don't think I need anything to put me to sleep." She snuggled down under the covers.

Her mother kissed her. "Good night, honey."

"Good night, Mom."

"Good night, Shane," she whispered.

* * * * *

"Well, Robin, do you have your skis waxed?" her father asked one evening at dinner. "I think we're going to be lucky this Thanksgiving vacation. The Sierra range just got three feet of snow."

Could it really almost be the end of November? Robin wondered. Time seemed to have gone crazy, like a spinning top going so fast. Then it would slow down, and it would seem forever that Shane had been in a coma.

Ever since last year, she and Shane had been planning for the four-day ski trip over the Thanksgiving holiday. But now, how could she even think about a ski trip? "I can't go, Dad. I can't be away that long."

Her father pushed his plate away and looked at her for a long time before he spoke. "Robin, we've had reservations for nearly a year. I'm even taking off early on Wednesday. Your mother and I have been looking forward to some time off."

"I know. You two go ahead. I don't mind staying here alone."

"We can't leave you for four days," her father said.

"But I have to see Shane every day," Robin insisted. "His parents count on my being there. He could come out of the coma at any minute."

Robin saw her parents exchange looks. "Robin," her father said, "I think you'd better start facing the fact that Shane may not ever get well."

"No! I won't listen. I'm staying home."

"You're going, and that's final," her mother said sharply.

"Mom, you promised. You said I could see Shane every day. I've been doing everything you told me. You lied. It's not fair!"

Her father set down his cup so hard that the coffee sloshed into the saucer. "You do not talk to your mother that way, young lady."

Robin jumped up from the table, knocking over her chair as she ran to her room. She flung herself down on the bed and punched her pillow. Angry tears welled to her eyes. "Shane is getting better," she said aloud. "I know it! I know it! It isn't fair to make me leave."

After a bit she walked over to the mirror and pulled off the scarf that hid Shane's words. *I LOVE YOU, ROBIN.*

"Oh, Shane," she said to herself, "everything's such a mess. I don't want Mom and Dad to be mad at me. Yeah, yeah, I know. You'd tell me to go apologize."

She brushed her hair and headed back to the dining room. At the door she heard her parents arguing because of her.

"We need to be here for her," her mother

was saying.

"Marian, we can't keep her wrapped in cotton for the rest of her life," her father said.

"What if Shane hadn't pushed her out of the way? Robin would be lying in a coma or. . . . George, one of us should have picked them up. If we had, none of this would have happened."

Robin crept back to her room and curled up on her bed. She leaned her head against the cold brass of the headboard. Mom's right, she thought. I should be the one in the hospital— not Shane.

A knock on the door startled her. She sat up quickly.

"May I come in?" her father asked.

She shrugged. "I guess."

He wandered around the room, looking at her collection of animals and hats. "Is this the same room I saw a couple of weeks ago? It's so neat. Did you hire a maid?"

Robin just shook her head.

He put on one of the baseball caps with S.F. GIANTS printed on it. "We haven't been to a game together for a long time." He flipped the cap, and it landed right on the hook. "I think the very first words out of your mouth were, 'Strike the bum out!' "

If he had come to bawl her out, she wished he'd get it over with.

He tried on a beanie that had a tiny propeller attached to the top. "Next time we go to a baseball game, how about if I borrow this?"

"Take any hat you want," she said. Except the pink one with the green feather, she thought.

He moved over to the dresser to look at himself in the mirror. "Now, this is"—as he stared at the words I LOVE YOU, ROBIN, she held her breath—"what I need," he finished.

He placed the beanie back on the peg, fingered the green feather on the crazy pink hat, then turned to Robin.

"Robin, honey, it won't be much of a Thanksgiving for you, but we'll see if we can find someone to stay with you."

"Oh, Daddy." She rushed over to her father. "Thank you." She flung her arms around him. "I love you. Thank you, thank you."

"Don't thank me yet. It'll be hard to find someone, you know."

"What about the McAllisters? I could stay with them. Holidays are going to be a bad time for them. I'll bet I can help them. May I go ask them right now before they go to the hospital?"

"All right. If it's okay with them and your

mother, it's fine with me. I'll talk to Mom."

Before he could change his mind, she grabbed Shane's jacket and hurried out the back door and across the lawn to the fence.

When she and Shane were little, they had made a hole under the fence so they could crawl into the other's yard. When the hole had gotten too big, her father had made a gate between the two houses.

She unlocked the gate, ran to the McAllisters' back door, and pounded loudly.

Shane's father answered. "Robin? What's wrong?"

Out of breath, she gasped. "Mom and Dad are going to the mountains for Thanksgiving. May I stay with you while they're gone? I don't want to miss my visits with Shane. Is it okay?"

"Sounds fine to me, but let's go in and ask Margaret. We were just on our way to the hospital."

Robin followed him into the living room where Mrs. McAllister was putting on her coat. "Robin, is something wrong?"

"No, I just have a favor to ask." Robin explained about the trip.

"We have the sofa bed in the family room," Mr. McAllister said to his wife. "And we sure don't have any plans."

"It's fine, dear," Shane's mother said. "But

I'm not planning to fix a turkey or any . . . "
Her voice choked and she turned away.

Mr. McAllister hurried to her side and put his arm around her.

"I don't care anything about turkey," Robin said softly. "I just want to be able to see Shane every day."

Mrs. McAllister turned around and smiled through her tears. "I think your being here will help us get through the holiday. And who knows, the two of us might whip up a pumpkin pie."

"Thanks," Robin said. "I really appreciate it. I promise I won't be any trouble."

Mrs. McAllister crossed the room and took Robin's face in her hands. "You could never be any trouble."

"Margaret," Mr. McAllister said quietly, "we'd better be going to the hospital."

Robin started to leave. At the door she said, "Tell Shane hello for me."

* * * * *

On Thanksgiving morning, Robin awakened early. For a moment, she didn't know where she was. She sat up quickly and knocked over a photograph on the end table. It was a picture of Shane when he was a Boy Scout. Luckily the glass hadn't broken. She looked at it for a long time, remembering him when he was eleven. That year he wouldn't even talk to her.

"Shane, you were a real jerk then," she whispered.

Hearing his parents in the kitchen, she quickly put the picture back on the table. She slipped on her robe and started to go across the hall to the bathroom when she overheard the McAllisters talking.

"Sam, how are we ever going to pay for all these hospital and doctor bills? It's running more than two thousand dollars a day. The insurance doesn't begin to pay for it."

"If we win the suit against the Haliburtons, we won't have to worry."

"But what if we lose? Besides Robin, there's only the one eyewitness, and she's seventy-nine and has a bad heart. What if she dies before the case comes to court?"

"Byron Elliot is trying to speed up the process and get the depositions taken as soon as possible. Honey, you let me worry about the money. I asked my boss to let me work over-time. If he won't, I'll get another part-time job."

Robin felt guilty. She'd been thinking only about her own pain, not how the McAllisters would pay for everything. Maybe there's something I can do about it, she thought. She cleared her throat and stepped into the kitchen.

Shane's mother was at the stove. Mr. McAllister was pouring orange juice.

"Good morning," Robin said, trying to sound cheerful. "What can I do to help?"

When Mrs. McAllister turned around, her eyes were red. "Good morning, dear. Did you sleep well? We're just having coffee, toast, and juice, but I can fix you—"

"Please, Mrs. McAllister, don't go to any extra work on my account. Toast and juice is fine."

The conversation at the breakfast table was strained.

"Robin, we're going to the hospital early today," Mr. McAllister said. "Do you want to come with us? We can take turns sitting with Shane."

"Oh, no. No, you go ahead. I'll go with you tonight."

"Are you sure?" Shane's mother asked. "I hate to leave you alone."

"That's okay. I'll watch the football games so I can tell Shane all about them."

"If you get hungry, there's tuna and bread," Mrs. McAllister told her. "I bought some frozen turkey dinners for tonight. I'm sorry.

It's not much of a Thanksgiving dinner, but . . ."

"Frozen dinners are just fine," Robin said quickly. "I like frozen dinners—especially turkey."

After breakfast Robin helped with the dishes, then she and Mrs. McAllister made a pie.

"How that boy loves pumpkin pie," Shane's mother said. "When Shane was little I had to watch him like a hawk." Her eyes brimmed with tears. "He was always drawing pictures in the whipped cream."

Seeing the pain on Mrs. McAllister's face, Robin's throat tightened. "He's going to be okay," Robin said. He has to, she thought.

Mrs. McAllister nodded. "I know, I know. I keep praying. But it's like I'm in a swamp, trying to wade through thick mud," she said to herself. "I'm so frustrated, and I feel so helpless. Nothing's happening. It just goes on and on and on." She stopped and bit her lip. "I'm sorry, Robin. It's just that I can't talk to anyone. They don't understand."

"I know. But we can't give up hope."

"You're right." She gave Robin a weak smile. "Now, let's go in and watch the Thanksgiving Day parade with Sam."

The three of them faced the television screen, but Robin was sure that none of them was really seeing the parade. She was glad when the McAllisters finally left for the hospital.

She wandered through the house, looking at the pictures of Shane, at things that he had touched. One door had a picture of the Olympic games in Los Angeles. It was Shane's room. She pushed open the door and stood in the doorway. She couldn't step in. She'd feel like a trespasser.

She hadn't seen his room since she was little, but it looked just like him. It was neat, but crowded with all his hobbies. A large drawing board stood near the window. His trophies and track ribbons, baseball bat, books, games, crazy signs, posters, cartoon sketches, and skis filled every inch of the room. She could almost imagine him sitting there at his desk. Any minute, he'd turn around and grin and say, "Hi, Robin."

She turned quickly away and closed the door. *Oh, Shane, come home. Please come home.*

Eight

ROBIN decided to fix a real Thanksgiving dinner for Shane's mom and dad. She knew there were three game hens in the freezer at home. She'd watched her mother prepare them with mandarin oranges and rice. It shouldn't be too hard.

She found a large can of fruit cocktail, some apples, oranges, bananas, and some imitation whipped cream. She mixed up a fruit salad and set it in the refrigerator. When she figured it was time to start the rest of the dinner, she basted the game hens with orange juice and soy sauce and put them in the oven. She couldn't find any instant rice, but Mrs. McAllister had some rice in a cannister. The only trouble was that there was no box with directions. Robin figured a cup of rice per person should do it. She filled a saucepan with water. When the water boiled, she added three cups of rice. While dinner cooked she went out to the living room to watch the football game.

After a while she smelled something burning and rushed back to the kitchen to find the rice flowing all over the stove and the floor. What had started out as three cups of rice, now looked like enough to feed everyone in China.

She was still cleaning up the mess when the McAllisters came home. Robin was almost in tears. "I'm so sorry. I thought I'd surprise you and have a nice dinner ready."

Mrs. McAllister's mouth twitched as if she were trying not to smile. "I think that was the nicest thing anyone has done for us. I'm sure the rest of the dinner will be wonderful. Almost as wonderful as our news."

"What news?" Robin asked. "Did Shane wake up? Is he better? Tell me, tell me."

"The doctor said Shane is breathing more on his own now. If he continues to improve and can breathe off the ventilator, he can be transferred to a regular ward."

Robin's insides were dancing. She wanted to jump up and down like a five-year-old. "That means he'll be out of the coma."

"No . . . They don't know how long that might take."

"But it might be today—or tomorrow." Robin wasn't going to let anything intrude on her joy. "I can't wait to tell the kids."

"It's certainly the best news we've had," Mr. McAllister said. "I think our prayers are going to be answered."

"We really have something to be thankful for," Robin said softly.

"You bet we have," Shane's mother said. "Now, let's get this kitchen cleaned up and dinner ready."

Mr. McAllister pitched in to help, and in no time they had the meal on the table.

Shane's mom and dad were the way they used to be, laughing and telling stories.

Mr. McAllister told one about when his mother had dropped the turkey when she was carrying it to the table. It had skidded across the kitchen, through the dining room door, and had stopped in front of the table. His mother picked it up, handed it to him and said, "Take this to the kitchen, Sammy, and bring out the 'other' turkey."

"I just stood there like a dummy until I realized she meant for me to bring back the same turkey." Mr. McAllister chuckled. "I wasn't too bright in those days."

Mrs. McAllister laughed. "Did Shane ever tell you about the time when he was five and we were so hard up we hadn't had any meat for a month?"

Robin shook her head. "He only talks about the good times."

"Well, it really wasn't so bad," Mr. McAllister said. "It made us appreciate things more."

"Anyway," Shane's mother went on, "I had saved up enough money to buy hot dogs for Thanksgiving dinner. Every day, I'd tell Shane what a wonderful dinner we were going to have—hot dogs. I made them sound like the best food in the world. I mean, his little tongue was drooling for hot dogs."

"Stop!" Robin said jokingly. "You're making me hungry for a hot dog."

"Shane was bragging to one of the neighbors about having hot dogs for Thanksgiving. He was excited about it, but Mrs. Stringfellow felt so sorry for the poor little boy. So on Thanksgiving, she came over with a beautiful baked chicken. You should have seen Shane." Mrs. McAllister laughed and shook her head. "His little face puckered up, and he began to cry. 'But Mama,' he sobbed, 'I want my hot dog!' "

"Oh, am I ever going to tease Shane—" She stopped. For a few minutes she had actually forgotten that Shane was lying in a coma.

"It's all right to laugh, Robin," Mr. McAllister said. "Shane would hate it if we all stopped living because of him."

No one said anything for a while. They finished eating in silence. "The dinner was delicious, Robin," Mrs. McAllister said. "I haven't had game hen in a long time."

"Game hen?" Mr. McAllister said, grinning. "Why, I thought they were little turkeys with stunted growth."

Robin helped clear the table. When they were eating the pumpkin pie, she remembered her earlier thought. "Uh, I have an idea—if it wouldn't make you mad or anything."

"What idea is that?" Mrs. McAllister asked.

"Well, I was thinking about starting a Shane McAllister fund—if it's okay with you."

"I don't approve of charity," Mr. McAllister said coldly.

"Shane has so many friends," Robin told him. "I'll bet all the kids in SADD would want to help. We could have car washes and bake sales and stuff like that." Robin stared down at her hands. "We'd like to help. It would make us feel closer to Shane."

Mrs. McAllister blinked rapidly. "I think it's a lovely thing to want to do." She looked at her husband. "What do you think, Sam?"

"I don't know—" he began.

"You could use the money to buy special things for Shane," Robin broke in. "And just like SADD, the fund might make other kids more aware of what drinking and driving can do."

"Well . . . I suppose it's all right. It's true we need to make people more aware of drunk driving." Mr. McAllister reached across the table and patted Robin's hand. "No wonder Shane thinks so much of you."

"Robin, dear, I don't think we've ever told you how proud we are the way you got the SADD chapter started at school."

A warm glow filled Robin. For the first time since the accident, she didn't feel useless, but as if she were accomplishing something worthwhile.

* * * * *

Thanksgiving vacation was over, and Robin was anxious to get back to work on SADD projects. She wanted to start a campaign of using posters to warn people about drinking and driving over the Christmas holidays. The first meeting was just a small group, not the entire membership. Robin decided to bring up the idea of a Shane McAllister fund.

She noticed Troy sitting in the back. It irked her that he came to all the meetings, but there wasn't much she could do about it. Well, see how he likes this, she thought.

"I have a great idea," she said to the group. "Let's start a Shane McAllister fund. His folks could really use some help. His medical bills are running more than $2,000 a day, and their insurance doesn't cover it all." She deliberately looked at Troy.

"Well, what do you think, guys?" Robin asked, looking around at everyone. "Isn't it a terrific idea? I'll bet we can raise a lot of money for Shane. Look how much we got on the SADD car wash."

"It sounds okay, I guess," Mike said. "But don't we have to get permission?"

"Yes, you will," Coach Adams said. "You should check with the city, the sheriff, and the Student Body. Mrs. Harvey, the Student Body Account Clerk, can handle the money part."

Robin looked at Cheryl and Jackie. "How about you two?"

Neither girl answered for a minute.

Robin sighed. She had thought they would be as excited as she was. She had nearly gone crazy over the long weekend. Jackie and Cheryl had both been out of town visiting their grandparents. Mike and Bob had been in the mountains skiing. As soon as her parents had come home, she had gotten their permission to start the Shane McAllister fund.

"I like the idea all right," Cheryl said, "but

the band is raising money for new uniforms, and the swim team needs money to go to meets next spring. I don't see how we'd do very well."

"And won't it spoil the things we're doing for SADD?" Jackie asked.

"I won't let it interfere. I'm going ahead," Robin said, trying not to show her hurt and anger, "with or without your help."

"For Pete's sake, Robin, you get so gung ho about everything to do for Shane or SADD," Bob told her. "Relax a bit."

"Right," Mike said. "Don't get all out of shape. We want to help Shane, too. What do you want us to do?"

"Tomorrow, I'm going to talk to the principal and see what all I have to do to get the fund started. But in the meantime, we could make posters and flyers. The more publicity we get, the better."

"I'll ask the art department if they'll take on that job," Bob offered.

"That's great," Robin said. "We can put one of Shane's cartoons on the flyer."

"I can help," Pat Erickson said. "WBY makes lots of public service announcements. I can plug all of your moneymaking projects."

"How about an auction?" Cheryl suggested. "We could gather up a bunch of stuff."

"I like that idea," Robin said. "I could bring some of Shane's cartoons. He has caricatures of old Ledbetter, some of the other teachers, the principal, and even some of the kids. I know Shane wouldn't mind."

"I'll bet they'd sell right off," Jackie said.

"Yeah," Bob said, "maybe we could make copies of the one of old Ledbetter. Every kid in school would buy one."

"If we could hold the auction just before Christmas, people would buy lots of things," Robin said.

Everybody groaned.

"That's too soon," Jackie said with a scowl. "There's too much to do around the holidays."

Robin guessed they were right about everybody being busy. "Okay, right after the first of the year, then. I'll get permission, and get the ball rolling."

As everyone was leaving, Robin stopped them. "Hey, guys," she said softly. "Thanks."

"No problem," Mike said. "Everyone in this room wants to help Shane."

Everyone? Robin wondered. She looked at Troy. There was no way he could help Shane. No way at all.

Nine

ROBIN tacked a SADD poster onto the bulletin board in the activity room. It was to remind everyone about drinking and driving over the Christmas holidays. As she bent over to reach for another poster, Coach Adams came in with a man. They were talking about Troy, and Robin realized they thought they were alone.

"Are you home for the holidays, Al?" Coach asked.

"I get home every Christmas. How'd you do this season?"

"We lost every game after the one you saw in October. Didn't you hear about the Haliburton kid?"

Not sure what to do, Robin stood glued to the spot.

"Sure," the man called Al said. "We were ready to offer him a football scholarship. Too bad. He had a lot of talent. But what about the McAllister boy? I want to take a look at him next year."

"I guess you haven't heard. It was Shane who was hit by Troy Haliburton. He's still in a coma."

"Aw, hey, that's a rotten shame. Do you think he'll be back soon?"

"I don't know if he'll ever be back," Coach said quietly.

"Lousy shame. The boy is a natural. Good hands. And fast."

"It doesn't look good," Coach said.

Robin stiffened. How could Coach say such a thing? Shane was getting better now. Soon, he'd be able to breathe without a ventilator. It might take him a while to get into shape, but he'd be back.

Quietly, she picked up the box of posters and slipped out the door.

*   *   *   *   *

A week before Christmas, Robin was eating dinner, and enjoying it for a change. Shane seemed to be breathing better now, and this was the first time she'd had an appetite since the accident.

She helped herself to another serving of

spaghetti. "This is great, Mom," she said. "It's the best you've ever made."

Her mother smiled. "It's the same recipe I always use."

"Mom, I've been wondering. What can I give Shane for Christmas this year? They don't allow anything in ICU."

Her mother shook her head. "That's a hard one. I don't know."

"What about a music tape?" her father suggested. "You said you think that he can hear you."

"I'd like it to be more personal," Robin said.

"So, play your guitar."

Robin made a face. "I haven't played it in ages. I'd make all the patients in ICU even sicker."

But why not make a tape of familiar sounds? Robin thought. "Mom, may I borrow your small recorder for the next few days?"

"I won't be using it. It's in my desk, and extra cassettes are in a box beside it."

That was one of the nice things about her parents—they never asked a lot of questions. "Thanks. I'll be careful with it."

As soon as she finished helping with the dishes, Robin got out the recorder and a blank sixty-minute cassette and took them to her room. She settled down on her bed and started to record.

"Merry Christmas, Shane. This is probably a crazy gift to you, especially since you might get out of ICU pretty soon. But it will help you remember all the good times we've had . . . and all the wonderful sounds in the world."

She switched off the recorder and put it in her jacket pocket so she wouldn't forget to take it when she went jogging.

It rained in the night, but the next morning was clear and fresh. Robin paused on the porch and switched on the recorder. "It's a beautiful morning, Shane—just the kind you like. You can't smell the damp earth, but listen to last night's rain dripping from the eaves."

She stood quietly for a minute, hardly breathing as she taped the sounds around her.

Several birds chattered and scolded. A frog gave a deep-throated *Ribb-ett.* From somewhere down the street came the sound of a motorcycle. A newspaper thunked onto the porch next door. A dog barked.

While she jogged she turned off the recorder. Otherwise, all Shane would hear would be the sound of her breathing. When she reached the lake, she sat on a bench for a few minutes and switched on the recorder. It's really neat, she thought. I never really heard all these sounds before—water dripping from the trees, birds scolding, the crunch of my footsteps on the gravel, the muffled roar of morning traffic in the distance, a radio playing rock music, a jet going overhead, the lapping of tiny waves against a log.

Robin didn't talk into the recorder, but when she got to school, she asked some of the kids to say something to Shane. She turned the recorder on again in the cafeteria and taped all the sounds. That evening she taped the Christmas carols that rang out from every store.

When the hour-long cassette was nearly used up, she said softly, holding the recorder close to her face. "Merry Christmas again, Shane. I hope you enjoy hearing this. I know I had fun making it. It reminded me of all the things we've done together, of all the things we'll do together soon. You've missed the football season, but as soon as you're well, we'll start getting into shape for track. I really miss you, Shane."

Her throat choked, and she could hardly get out the last words. "Please wake up. The best Christmas present I could ever have would be for you to come out of that coma. Shane, please, please wake up."

* * * * *

On December 24th Robin woke up to a white world. She couldn't even remember the last time it had snowed in Woodbridge.

I'm going to get Shane, she thought, and we'll build a crazy snowman and . . . then she remembered.

She closed the curtains and wandered out to the living room. In the daylight the Christmas tree no longer looked beautiful.

The last few weeks she'd been so busy with SADD and the Shane fund that time had gone swiftly. But because Shane wasn't out of the hospital, she felt a little down.

She slumped onto the floor in front of the tree and fingered one of the shiny ornaments. It was one that Shane had made for her last year. On it was a cartoon of a girl on skis, or rather of a girl lying in the snow with her skis in the air.

I almost wish we hadn't put up a tree this year, she thought. Shane can't even have a poinsettia or any decorations in ICU.

"What's the matter, honey?"

She looked up to see her father standing in the doorway.

"I don't know. I just feel sad for some reason."

He came in and sat on the arm of the couch. "Lots of people feel that way during the holidays. You've had two months of uncertainty and worry over Shane. It's natural to be depressed."

"It's like Shane's mom said. It just goes on and on, and you feel so helpless. If I could just do something."

"I know," he said. "You don't remember my father. He had a stroke when I was just about your age. I felt guilty that maybe it was my fault somehow. I felt guilty because I'd never really told him how much I loved him." Her father gave a deep, quivering sigh. "He died before I could let him know."

"I'm sorry, Daddy." She reached up and kissed him. "I love you."

"I know you do. And I know my father knew I loved him, too. And I'm sure Shane knows how much you and everyone else cares for him."

"Sometimes I'm sure he does. Other times . . ."

"I get off early today. If you want to go to the hospital this evening before dinner, I'll take you."

"Thanks. I'd like that. I think I'll give Shane his Christmas present. His parents will stay with him all day tomorrow. And, Dad, thanks for telling me about Grandpa."

"You won't believe it now, but all pain eases

with time."

During the day, the snow turned to dirty slush. It was dark when Robin and her father drove to the hospital.

"I'll pick you up in the lobby in an hour," her father told her. "I still have some last-minute Christmas shopping to do."

As Robin headed to Shane's wing, she passed a group of carolers.

Last year, she and Shane had gone out caroling. It isn't fair that anyone has to be in the hospital at Christmas.

She stopped at the nurses' station to ask how Shane was doing.

"He's holding his own," she was told. "You can go right in."

"I made a tape for him. It runs an hour, and I only have fifteen minutes. Is it all right if I leave it on when I leave?"

"Of course," the nurse said. "I'll put the recorder away when the tape is finished."

Robin thanked her and went into Shane's room. He looked thinner than ever. She took out the pink hat. The green feather was limp and faded. She put Rabbit on the bed beside Shane, then she turned on the tape player.

Her voice blared out, and she turned down the volume.

"Merry Christmas, Shane. This is a crazy

gift to give you, especially since you might be out of ICU pretty soon . . . ."

Until her time was up, Robin listened to the tape. If only he would give some sign that he could hear it.

She picked up Rabbit, held it to her face, and pretended it was Rabbit talking. "Merry Christmas, Shane, ol' buddy, ol' pal. You'd better get well in a hurry now. You hear? Robin overheard a scout from one of the colleges talking to Coach Adams. He has his eye on you. So, you'd better get out of this place. You hear?"

She put the hat and Rabbit back into her bag and got up quietly. As she went out the door, she heard Mike's voice on the tape. "Shane, old buddy, we're all rooting for you. It's not the same around here without you. Stop goofing around and get back home. Okay?"

"Yes, Shane," Robin whispered, "stop goofing around."

As she came out, she ran into the McAllisters. "Hi, I didn't expect you so soon," Robin said.

"We got off work early," Mrs. McAllister said. "Merry Christmas, dear."

"You too, only I know it's not very happy for you."

"Well, someone got a nice Christmas

present," Mr. McAllister said grimly. "We just heard that Troy Haliburton got off easy—five years of probation and he loses his driver's license for one year." His voice was harsh. "Some punishment for what he's done to Shane!"

Anger started in Robin's head and feet and spread inward, meeting in her stomach in one quivering, aching mass. She wanted to smash something, throw something, strike out. She wanted to do something. He won't get away with this, she thought. God won't let him get away with it.

Ten

"HEY, everybody, have I got great news." Robin looked around the room at the kids who were working on the auction. "Mrs. Harvey said we got a cashier's check from an anonymous donor for a thousand dollars. Can you believe it? A thousand bucks! That means we've already raised thirty-two hundred."

With the newspaper and radio follow-up stories about how long Shane had been in a coma, the bake sales and car washes brought in more money than anybody had expected. But Robin was really surprised at how many checks had come in from people who had heard about Shane and wanted to help.

"Okay, let's go over the plans for the auction," she said. "Mike, do you have the flyers and posters yet?"

"Right here." He lifted a box onto the table.

Robin lifted one out. "Wow! These are great. They look like they're professionally made."

Mike didn't look at her. "They are," he mumbled.

"Oh, no, you didn't spend a lot of money on them, did you?"

Mike look uncomfortable. "They didn't cost us a cent."

"You'd better tell her," Bob said. "She's bound to find out."

Robin looked from one to the other and frowned. "I'll find out what? You couldn't have stolen them."

"I gave the job to the senior who helped make the SADD posters. Now, don't get upset. He said Troy—"

"Troy!" Robin broke in. "What's he got to do with this?"

"I knew you were going to have a fit," Mike said. "Troy had them made at a professional printer."

Robin bit back a bitter remark. It galled her that he was trying to horn in on the auction. Did he think he could make up for what he'd done by paying for a few posters and flyers?

"I think it was pretty nice of him," said one of the junior girls in charge of publicity.

Robin managed to control her anger and

went through the rest of the plans.

"Pat's given us so much coverage on the radio, I'll bet the auditorium won't hold everyone," Robin said. "Bob, are you sure we'll have enough chairs?"

"Plenty. And Harris Moving Company said they'd bring in any large items that people donate for the auction."

"Cassie, how are the jumpsuits coming? Will they be ready in time?"

"Sure. The Home Ec class is embroidering Shane's name on the back."

Robin, Cheryl, Jackie, Bob, and Mike were to bring out the things to be auctioned. They would all be wearing the green jumpsuits over their clothes.

"Good." Robin turned to Jackie. "Who did you put in charge of finding an auctioneer?"

"Brooke Halston," Jackie said quickly, too quickly.

Robin caught the look between Jackie and Cheryl. A sinking cold settled in her stomach. "And who did she get? Someone who auctions off livestock?" She tried to make it sound like a joke, but the sinking feeling got worse.

"Actually, it's a guy who auctions off stuff at estate sales—you know, when someone dies. He's supposed to be really good."

"And how much is he charging us?"

"Nothing, nothing at all. He's doing it—for nothing," Jackie said lamely.

Robin nodded slowly. "And I'll bet this auctioneer knows the Haliburtons." She hit the table with her fist. "What right does Troy have to butt in on this fund for Shane! He's using his money and pull to make everybody think he's a nice guy. I hate—"

"Take it easy." Cheryl walked over to Robin. "What harm does it do to use the posters and the auctioneer? We need all the help we can get."

Robin pulled away and hurried out to the hall. She leaned her head against the wall, trying to stop shaking. Everywhere she turned, it was Troy. Troy. Troy!

After a few minutes she returned to the meeting. "Okay," she said, "you're right, we can use all the help we can get. So, let's get busy. We have only two more weeks to get ready for this auction."

* * * * *

When Robin was dressing to go to the auction, she was so excited she was half sick. Her stomach felt like a dryer spinning her insides around.

Her mother came into the room. "Robin?

It's almost time to leave." They were going early and meeting the McAllisters at the school.

Robin's mother was wearing a brown wool and silk suit with a beige blouse. "You look great, Mom."

"Thanks, honey. And you look cute in that green jumpsuit," her mother said.

"I don't feel cute. I'll bet my face looks as green as my outfit."

On the way to the auditorium, Robin worried about all the things that could go wrong. She wanted everything to be perfect for Shane.

When they arrived, girls from Shane's homeroom handed them a list of the larger or more expensive items to be auctioned. Robin looked around for the McAllisters. "I guess they're not here yet," she said.

"We'll watch for them," her dad said. "You go on and do what you have to do."

"Okay," she said. "We have reserved seats for you and Shane's parents right down front. But don't let on that you're part of the program."

"Stop worrying," her mother said. "It's all going to go off perfectly."

"Oh, I hope so. I'll meet you when it's all over."

The auditorium looked festive. Dozens of baskets of flowers and plants decorated the stage. They all had been donated by florists to be auctioned off. The larger donations were displayed on the stage and below it.

As Robin looked for her friends, she felt a tap on her arm. She looked down to see a small boy.

"Are you the girl who's raising money for Shane McAllister?"

Robin nodded. The boy looked familiar, but she couldn't place him. "I sure am, along with a lot of other people."

"Shane gave me some tickets at the carnival 'cause I lost mine."

"Sure. I remember you now. You were afraid your brother was going to kill you." Robin smiled. "I'm glad to see he didn't."

The boy dug in his pocket and pulled out a quarter, a nickel, and six pennies. "This is all I got, but I want to give it to Shane. Oh, and this, too." He dug in another pocket and held out a toy car. "For the auction tonight."

Robin was so touched she wanted to hug the boy, but she knew he'd hate that. Instead she took the money and the car. "Thank you very much," she said solemnly. "Shane will really appreciate it."

Robin watched the boy run off, then she

116

hurried to join her friends by a table piled high with every imaginable item. "Here's something else to sell," she said and held up the car.

"Look at all this stuff," Robin said, shaking her head in awe.

"Hey, Robin," one of the sophomore ushers said, "get a load of this VCR and stereo set. Troy brought it in just a little while ago. It looks almost brand new. I'll bet it cost a thousand bucks."

A cold fury swept over Robin, but without a word, she spun on her heel and walked to her chair at the foot of the stage. *I won't let Troy spoil this evening. I won't. I won't.*

Cheryl and Jackie joined Robin just as Mr. Jackson, the principal picked up the microphone. He was serving as the master of ceremonies for the evening. When he finished his little speech, he introduced the auctioneer, a tall thin man with a deep, powerful voice like an actor.

At first the items didn't bring too much, but as the auction went on, even the junk was bringing a high price. Robin bought the little red car for five dollars. Shane's drawings that she had donated were some of the last things to be auctioned. Robin almost withdrew one of his favorites, though. It was a large exaggerated sketch of her on skis, wrapped around a tree.

After auctioning off a number of the drawings which had brought ten or fifteen dollars each, the auctioneer read another name on the back of a sketch. "We have here a drawing of a teacher—a Mr. Ledbetter." He looked at the sketch and laughed. "It's not exactly flattering, so we'll start the bid at five dollars."

The bidding was spirited. It finally went to Mr. Ledbetter himself for fifty dollars.

Robin whispered to Cheryl, "Maybe old Ledbetter's not so bad, after all."

The auctioneer picked up the next sketch. "This one is titled 'Robin.' She seems to be climbing a tree with skis on. What am I bid?"

Robin sighed. "I wish I'd kept that one," she said to Jackie. "It won't bring nearly as much as the teachers' sketches."

From the crowd, she heard a bid of twenty-five dollars. Another voice called thirty. "I hear thirty, thirty, do I hear thirty-five?"

She couldn't see who was bidding in the back, but then she recognized her father's voice. "Forty dollars," he said.

The voice way in the back row called out, "Fifty!"

"I have fifty—fifty—fifty once—"

Robin's father yelled, "Sixty!"

"Hey, your dad is really something," Mike said. "Mine wouldn't pay a dime for a picture of me."

"I wish he wouldn't," Robin said. "That's too much money."

Cheryl was peering out, trying to see. "I wonder who that is bidding against your dad?"

The bidding went back and forth until the price was up to seventy-five dollars. "Sold," the auctioneer said, "for seventy-five dollars to the gentleman in the first row."

She went to her father and hugged him. "Daddy, you shouldn't have, but thank you. How did you know I really wanted to keep that picture?"

"I saw your face when the sketch went on the auction block. I didn't expect to have to outbid somebody else. But it's for a good cause."

Robin went back to her friends. "Could any of you see who was bidding against my dad?" Robin asked.

"I did," Mike told her. "It was Troy."

They all looked at Robin. She didn't say a word, but inside she was seething. If I hear his name, one more time tonight, I'm going to scream, she thought. Then as if fate were punishing her for something, the next item to be auctioned was Troy's VCR and stereo system.

That does it, she thought. As the bidding began, Robin made her way to the back of the auditorium. She came up behind Troy just as he bid four hundred on his own VCR.

"Well, at least there was one thing your money couldn't buy," she said.

Troy turned around. His face blanched, and he tried to move away.

"Oh, no you don't! You've been avoiding me. You haven't even had the guts to face Shane," she taunted. "Now, you're going to listen to me." Her voice was shrill, and people were turning to look at them. But Robin didn't care any more.

"I'm glad my dad outbid you. I'd rather die than see you have that sketch! You think giving money pays for everything, don't you." Her voice was low and deadly cold. "Oh, you'll pay, all right, Troy, but not with money."

His face looked as if she'd struck him. "I'm sorry, Robin. I'm sorry." He turned and headed for the exit.

"Aren't you going to buy back your VCR?" she called after him.

He ducked out the door.

She walked on outside. The air was cold, and it felt good on her hot face. After a few minutes, Cheryl came out.

"Robin, you shouldn't let Troy get to you that way. He isn't worth it."

"I know. Whenever I see him or even hear his name, I see his car bearing down on us, and I . . ." She angrily brushed away the tears that had sprung to her eyes. "I'm sorry. I wanted this evening to be perfect for Shane and his parents."

"It is. It's a great success. Now, come on in. Mr. Jackson has already introduced the McAllisters."

When they came back inside, the principal was handing Shane's mother and father a check for $9,784.

There was loud applause.

Mr. Jackson raised his hand and shouted over the noise, "And that's not counting what the auction brought in tonight."

There was another roar of applause.

He grinned ruefully. "I have to admit I'm a little put out, though, about the bidding tonight. Shane's picture of me didn't bring in as much money as Robin Nichols' or Mr. Ledbetter's."

Everyone laughed, but both of Shane's parents looked as if they were going to cry. Mr. McAllister's voice shook as he thanked the principal, then turned to face the crowd.

"I don't have the words to express our thanks for everyone's kindness and generosity." He put his arm around his wife. "All we can say is—thank you." He held up the check. "This will go a long way in helping our boy—" His voice broke completely then, and he pulled out a handkerchief to wipe his eyes.

Mrs. McAllister spoke then. "We'd like to especially thank someone who's very close to Shane. She's the one who came up with the idea of the fund. Robin?" Mrs. McAllister looked straight at Robin. "Thank you for everything you've done."

Tears stung Robin's eyes. She stood up and faced the crowd. "Thank you. But it wasn't me, it was all of you. Shane will be able to thank you himself very soon."

She sat down to the sound of thunderous applause.

* * * * *

It was too late to visit Shane that night, but Robin went to see him the next morning. She stopped at the nurses' station to ask if it was okay to go in now.

"I'm sorry, Robin," the nurse told her. "Shane's developed pneumonia."

"Oh, no! How serious is it?"

"Well, we don't know yet. We've just given him a lot of medication."

"May I just go in for a minute? I have something I want to give him."

"All right, but just a minute."

Robin slipped into his room. She looked at him closely. Except that his breathing was faster, she couldn't see any change.

"Shane, I can't stay now, so I'll tell you all about the auction next time I come to see you."

She took the little red car from her bag and held it up to Shane. "Do you remember the boy at the carnival? He was the one who'd lost his tickets. Well, he came to the auction tonight and donated some money and this little car. He was so cute and so proud to do something for you.

"Shane? Do you have any idea how many people care about you?" Her voice broke. "Especially me," she whispered.

Eleven

FEBRUARY dragged by. It rained more than usual, and sometimes Robin felt as dismal as the weather.

One Friday evening, Shane's mother called Robin. "I thought you'd want to know, dear. Tomorrow, the doctors are going to give Shane another brain scan and an EEG."

"Why? What's wrong?" Robin's heart took a dive. "Oh, Mrs. McAllister, he's not worse, is he?"

"No, but he's not responding the way he should. They want to check the brain activity and to see if there's bleeding in the brain." Robin could tell by Mrs. McAllister's voice that she was trying to control her emotions. "If there is bleeding, they may have to operate."

"Will it hurt him—this scan thing?"

"I don't think so." Shane's mother said. "The CAT scan will show what's happening in the brain." Her voice harshened. "They can do all kinds of things, but they can't bring him out of a coma." Her voice rose. "He's been lying there for months, and the doctors haven't done a—"

Mr. McAllister came on the line. "I'm sorry, Robin. She's pretty upset. We'll see you tomorrow at the hospital."

Robin set the phone down gently and sank onto the couch. Fear, like a band of metal, squeezed her chest. *Bleeding in the brain. An operation.* For the first time since the accident, she was afraid, afraid that Shane might not make it, that he might—die. She didn't even want to think that word.

She picked up the phone again and called Cheryl. She explained about the tests and possible operation. "Will you call Jackie, Mike, and Bob and see if they want to go to the hospital tomorrow?"

"Sure. It's Saturday. We'll be there."

That night, Robin slept very little. She kept waking up with vague feelings of terror, as of a half-remembered nightmare. She was up at first light. By the time she started jogging, the creamy sky was turning a rosy gold. The dew glistened like pink diamonds. As she ran across the yard, her feet made a silver swath in the grass.

How could anything bad happen on such a beautiful morning?

* * * * *

Mike looked up at the clock in the hospital cafeteria. "It's been nearly two hours."

"Is that all?" Bob asked. "It feels like we've been waiting for a year."

"Maybe they had to operate," Jackie said. "My grandfather was on the table for six hours."

"Six hours!" Cheryl groaned. "I'll go nuts if we have to wait that long."

Robin drank the last of her hot chocolate, which was now cold and scummy. She crumbled the styrofoam cup, and the loud snap startled all of them. "Sorry," she said. "Maybe we should go back to the waiting room. Shane's mom and dad might have heard something by now."

"I'd rather stay here," Mike said. "The waiting room gives me the creeps."

"Me, too," Bob said. "That lady who was crying because her husband just died really got to me." He shivered. "I hate hospitals."

"Somebody will come to get us," Mike said. He shook his head slowly. "I can't get over how thin Shane is. I don't see how he'll ever get back in shape in time for track."

"It gets me the way he just lies there," Jackie said. "I don't think I ever saw him sit still for five minutes—before . . ."

"Yeah," Bob said with a little laugh. "He had more energy than all the rest of us put together."

"Remember a couple of years ago when he broke his foot?" Jackie grinned. "He was hopping around like a one-legged rabb—" She stopped, realizing that Robin was holding Rabbit in her arms.

Mike broke in quickly. "Anybody want some more chocolate or a roll or anything?"

"Just some water," Robin said. "My mouth feels like I've been eating cotton balls."

Mike brought her a cup of water. She took a sip, but it tasted bitter.

"Remember when Ledbetter put Shane on detention because he brought one of those seaweed bulbs full of water to class?" Mike asked.

Robin's mind jumped to the time she and Shane had a water fight. He'd squirted her in the face with a water pistol. "Gotcha!" Shane had yelled.

"You rat! That's not fair," she had said. "I don't have a pistol."

He got her again, and sputtering and laughing,

she grabbed a glass of water.

"Oh, no, you don't," he cried and headed for the door. She threw the water. In trying to duck, he hit the door with an awful bang.

"Shane, I'm sorry." He was holding his face. "Are you okay?"

"I think I'm going to have a black eye."

"Let me see." He took his hand away, and she gasped. "Oh, no! You must have hit the bridge of your nose. Both eyes are beginning to swell."

He grinned painfully. "I guess it's my own fault. I started it."

"Well, I didn't mean to end it that way."

Then her lips began to twitch. "You look so funny." She couldn't keep from smiling. "With those two black eyes, you look like a panda or a raccoon." Then she had begun to laugh. "The kids won't believe you got two black eyes from hitting a door."

Robin looked up now and realized the kids were watching her. "I was just thinking about something funny that Shane, that he—I have to go find out what's happening to him."

She pushed back her chair to stand and nearly fell. She gave a little laugh. "My legs feel all weak and quivery."

"You don't look so hot," Mike said. "You've lost weight, haven't you?"

"A little, I guess."

"I wish I could," Jackie said. "I gained four pounds over Christmas vacation. Some people have all the luck."

Sure, Robin thought, some people have all the luck.

"Anybody coming with me?" Robin asked.

The boys stayed behind. As Robin, Cheryl, and Jackie were riding up the elevator to the neurological section, Cheryl said, "If Shane doesn't need an operation, I think I'll go on home. I have a piano lesson at eleven-thirty."

"Sure," Robin said. "We probably won't know much right away, anyhow."

Jackie made a face. "I kind of hate to ask this, but—well, will they be able to tell if he has brain damage?"

"I don't know," Robin said.

"I've heard of people who stay in comas for years. Boy, I think I'd rather be dead than be like a veg—" Jackie began.

Robin cut her off. "He's going to be fine!"

"I'm sorry, Robin, but that's how I feel."

The elevator stopped, and a young man in white pants and coat stepped in. He smiled at them, then read some papers he was carrying. When he got off on the next floor, Jackie pretended to faint.

"Wasn't he gorgeous? I'd go to the doctor

every day if he looked like that hunk."

Robin turned on her. "How can you even think about guys when they may be operating on Shane right now?"

"We're just as worried about him as you are," Jackie said. "But I'm not going to stop living. Everybody at school thinks you're nuts to go see him every day. For gosh sakes, it's not like he even knows you're there."

"He does know it!" Robin cried. "And if he's in a coma for fifty years, I'll still come to see him every day."

Tears stung at Robin's eyes. Shane's mom was right, she thought angrily. Nobody really understands.

They were silent as they made their way to the waiting room. Mrs. McAllister jumped up and hurried to meet them.

"Good news," she said. "They aren't going to operate." She smiled weakly. "I didn't realize how worried I was."

"Did the doctor say anything?" Robin asked. "Do they know why he hasn't come out of the coma?"

Mr. McAllister shook his head. "When we visit Shane tomorrow evening, the doctor will tell us what they've found out."

Robin sighed. More waiting. Always, it was more waiting.

* * * * *

The next day, Robin, her mother, and the McAllisters had been waiting in the lounge for the doctor to give them the results of Shane's tests.

Robin stood up. "I'm going to peek in for just a minute and see how Shane's doing. Is it okay?"

Shane's parents nodded.

"Don't be long," Robin's mother told her.

Robin hurried down the corridor to Shane's room. She wanted to tell him about the Valentine party SADD was sponsoring. They planned to sell carnations with a tag that said, "Friends Don't Let Friends Drive Drunk."

The door was partially open, but there was no one by Shane's bed. Robin went on in. "Hi, Shane. I only have a minute, but I just wanted—"

She stopped as she heard a strangled cry, almost a moan. She turned to see Troy, his face paste-white, stunned, backed up against the wall.

Cold anger took the blood from her face. "What are you doing in Shane's room?" she hissed.

He swallowed convulsively. His lips moved, but no words came out.

"I said, what are you doing in here!" she cried. She moved toward him. "What right have you got to be in this room? Get out!" she shouted. "Get out!"

"I'm sorry," he whispered, not looking at her.

"Haven't you done enough? Get out!"

"Robin," her mother said from the door, "I heard you shout—"

She saw Troy then. "Robin, what's going on?"

"It's Troy. Make him get out of here!"

"Ssh, this is a hospital," her mother said and glanced toward Shane. "I think you'd better leave, Troy."

His shoulders slumped, and his legs looked as if he could hardly stand. "I'm sorry."

Troy moved slowly toward the door. He stopped and turned back and looked at Shane. He kept shaking his head. "I'm sorry."

Sorry. Sorry. Robin's shoulders trembled. *He was sorry!*

"Robin, we'd better go. You don't want to miss the doctor." Her mother led her back to the lounge.

Dr. Webber was just coming out of the elevator. The doctor was wearing green scrubs. A mask hung from his neck. "Sorry to keep you folks waiting," he said. "I had an emergency operation." His mouth tightened in a grim line. "Another drunk driver."

"What about Shane?" Mrs. McAllister asked. "What did you find out?"

"Not very much. The CAT scan showed no bleeding. And the EEG shows brain activity. We can't really see any reason why he isn't responding better."

Mrs. McAllister asked the question uppermost in Robin's mind.

"What about brain damage? Can you tell if he—if he . . ." Her voice trailed off.

"Unfortunately, we can't tell for sure. The fact that he's breathing on his own also shows us that there is brain activity. But I think you have to understand that it's unlikely he'll be the same as he used to be. The longer he's in a coma, the worse his chances."

Robin felt as if she'd been struck in the stomach with a baseball bat. She let out a little gasp. The doctor's words filled her head like a broken record. *It's unlikely that he'll be the same as he used to be.*

Mrs. McAllister looked at her. "Robin, are you all right?"

Robin's hand flew to her mouth. "I—I need to—I'll wait for my dad in the lobby."

"Robin? Don't—" Mr. McAllister began.

"I have to go." Robin almost ran from the

waiting room and hurried down the corridor. She sagged against the wall. Her very worst fears had become a reality. The Shane she had known for so long would never come back.

Her shoulders began to shake, and she could no longer hold back the tears.

Robin's mother came up and took Robin in her arms. "Let it out, honey. It's all right. It's all right."

Robin sobbed great wracking sobs that shook her body. She cried until there were no more tears. She cried until she felt weak and empty. She drew in a long shuddering breath, then hiccupped.

Her mother handed her a tissue. "Feel better now?"

Robin wiped her eyes and blew her nose. "I don't know why I broke down like that."

"It's normal to feel depressed and angry and frustrated. But something else is bothering you."

Robin unfolded the tissue and tore it into tiny bits. "I—I didn't know—the doctor said he'd probably never be the same Shane ever again . . . ."

"Robin, he said probably, not absolutely. There's always hope."

Robin blinked back tears and sniffed. "I'm not going to cry again!" she said. "It isn't fair! It just isn't fair!"

Twelve

FINALLY, in March, Shane improved enough to breathe on his own. He was taken off the ventilator. On the same day he was to be transferred to a regular room, Robin received a subpoena to give a deposition in the civil suit of the McAllisters against the Haliburtons.

As soon as her parents came home, she handed her mother the subpoena. "Mom, does this mean I have to testify in court?"

Her mother read through the document. "Eventually, you probably will, but this is just the discovery process to find out what really happened. It's what I do every day—take statements from witnesses in civil suits."

"Good, then you can be there with me. You can take my deposition."

"No. It would be improper for me to do that. In fact, I don't think I should even be there.

I've done work for both attorneys."

"But, Mom, I can't go alone. It's at one o'clock on a Tuesday, and Dad has to work."

"I'll take the time off," her father said.

"I don't see why they want to question me. I told the police I didn't really see anything. Do I have to go?"

"Of course you do," her mother said. "I'll tell you what to expect. It won't be bad at all."

But even with her mother's coaching, Robin was nervous when she entered Mr. Elliot's office. A secretary sat at a desk in a small, dingy waiting room.

Her father held out the subpoena. "Miss Robin Nichols was called to make a deposition."

The secretary was old and skinny and as dingy looking as the office. Robin hoped the lawyer was more impressive than what she'd seen so far.

"You'll have to wait out here, Mr. Nichols," the secretary told him. "Robin, come with me. They're waiting for you."

Robin gave her dad a scared look and followed the woman into a larger, but even drabber office. There were no windows, and a layer of smoke drifted toward the door.

An old man with stooped shoulders and a bush of yellowish-white hair and beard stood up. "Come in, child." Robin hesitated. "There's nothing to worry about," he said kindly. "We're just going to ask you a few questions."

He introduced her to a Mrs. Spinoza, the deposition reporter, and to the other lawyer, a Mr. Thompson. Robin mumbled a how-do-you-do.

"Mrs. Spinoza, will you swear in the witness, please?" Mr. Elliot asked.

Robin started to stand up. "That's not necessary," Mrs. Spinoza told her. "Just raise your right hand."

Mrs. Spinoza raised hers, too. "Do you solemnly swear that the testimony you shall give in this matter shall be the truth, the whole truth, and nothing but the truth, so help you God?"

Robin mumbled, "I do."

"What was your answer?"

Robin cleared her throat. "I do." It came out so loud it startled everyone in the room. "I'm sorry. I do."

"Miss Nichols," Mr. Elliot said. "Will you please state your full name and address for the record."

"Robin Sara Nichols. I live at 3540 Mission Street in Woodbridge, California."

"Robin, have you ever had a deposition

taken before?" the lawyer asked.

"No, but my mom takes depos every day. I know what they are."

"Good. A lawsuit is now pending between the Samuel McAllisters, the plaintiffs, and the defendants, Mr. and Mrs. Austin Haliburton. We are going to be asking you questions about an accident that occurred on October 14th of last year.

"It is important that you consider each question carefully, because the information you give us will be taken down in a brief booklet and presented to you for review.

"If you don't know the answer, don't guess. Tell us you don't know the answer. And one other thing. I will ask you not to interrupt while I am speaking. Mrs. Spinoza can only take down one speaker at a time." He smiled. "She starts tearing out her hair when two people talk at once.

"Also, the oath you have taken is the same oath you would take in a court of law. Do you understand?"

Robin nodded, worrying now about even remembering the events of that night in October.

"Please answer with a yes or no. Mrs. Spinoza's machine cannot take down nods of the head."

"I'm sorry," Robin said. Her mother had already warned her about that, too. "I forgot. Yes, I do understand."

"All right. Now, will you tell us your date and place of birth."

Robin answered the simple questions and began to feel more at ease. As truthfully as she could remember, she described the events leading up to the accident, then the crash itself.

It wasn't as hard to talk about now, and she thought she had done a good job. "May I go now?" she asked.

"Not yet," Mr. Elliot said. "Mr. Thompson, the attorney for the defense, will ask a few questions now."

Robin's stomach knotted. Mr. Thompson had a deep line in his forehead that made him look angry all the time.

"Remember, Miss Nichols, you are still under oath."

Robin nodded, then remembered the instructions. "I mean, yes, I know."

The lawyer went through a few simple questions, then he asked, "What was the weather like the evening of October 14th?"

Robin closed her eyes for a minute, remembering running from the gym. "It was raining."

"Hard?"

"No, just medium. I guess."

"You guess?"

"It was raining medium hard, and we were getting pretty wet."

"You have stated you left the high school gymnasium at approximately four-thirty to catch a bus only two blocks away. The accident happened at five. What did you do during that half hour?"

"Just waited. Two or three buses went by, but they were full."

"And what were you and Shane McAllister doing while you waited?"

"Talking."

"Talking? About what?"

"What difference does that make?" She looked at Mr. Elliot, but he was writing something down.

"Just answer the question, Miss Nichols. What were you talking about?"

Robin groaned to herself. "We were having a silly argument over a hat he'd won at the carnival."

"A silly argument? Were you shouting?"

"No, of course not. We were talking loud."

"Then all of your attention was on each other, not on the skidding car. Isn't that correct?"

Robin hesitated. Her mother had warned

her that the Haliburton's lawyer might try to put her and Shane in the wrong. "Y—es."

"Then we can assume that if you had not been arguing, you could have moved out of the way?"

"I don't know. It—it all happened so fast."

"All right. We'll come back to that later."

"Well, you sure don't expect a car on the sidewalk!"

He asked some more questions about how dark it was, the condition of the street, what she and Shane were wearing. Then he asked, "Do you normally take the bus at that time of the evening?"

"No. My mom or my dad usually pick me up. But they both had to work that day."

"And Shane's parents? Could you have called them to come pick you up?"

"No. They work even longer hours than my parents."

"Did your parents tell you when they would be home from work?"

"No, they never know exactly."

Now he's trying to make our parents out to be bad, Robin thought. A surge of anger flared through her. "People take buses all the time. But they don't expect to get hit by a drunk driver!"

"Please just answer my questions," the

141

lawyer said, ignoring her outburst.

"So, it's possible that they might have already been home. Did you try to call anybody when you saw how crowded the buses were on such a nasty night?"

"No."

"Were you aware that there was a telephone only a few yards from the bus stop?"

"No. We didn't even think of calling anyone."

"All right. Now, let's go back to the moment before the accident. You and the young man were arguing—about a hat?"

He made it sound so stupid. "Yes."

He took her through the horror of the oncoming car, the terrible sound of metal, the pain. "I've told you this before!" Robin cried. "How many times do I have to—"

"That's all for today, Miss Nichols. We appreciate your cooperation. You will see a copy of your deposition later."

Robin let out her breath slowly. Will I have to go through this all over again in court? she wondered. Shane, I hope I did all right. I sure wish you'd been here, too.

Mr. Elliot led her to the door. "You did very well, my dear. Thank you."

Robin felt drained and exhausted as she walked slowly to the waiting room. I blew it, she thought. I wasn't any help to Shane's folks.

Her father dropped the magazine he was reading and stood up. "How'd it go—pretty bad, huh?" he asked, putting his arm around her.

Robin leaned against him for a second. "I'm just a little tired, and I feel so—so helpless."

"Well, I'll take you right home—"

"I can't. I have an important SADD meeting at three-thirty. Just drop me off at school. I'll take the bus to the hospital after my meeting."

"Aren't you too tired for all that?"

"Shane's out of ICU now, and I can stay longer than fifteen minutes. I can rest there. I want to tell Shane about the deposition."

"All right. But don't stay too long. Be home before dark."

Remembering the lawyer's questions, Robin smile weakly. "Don't worry. If it's dark, I'll phone."

The SADD meeting was already going on when Robin arrived. Mike, as vice president, was running things. Every chair was filled. Robin couldn't help feeling a surge of pride at how large the working group had grown. And the total membership was up to nearly sixty-five percent of the student body.

Mike was talking about the possibility of having a membership competition between

Woodbridge High and their rival, Benson High. In January, with Pat Erickson's help, Benson had started a SADD chapter, too.

"We could have a prize for the first school to reach one hundred percent," Mike was saying. "Anybody have any ideas?"

"Maybe we could get some local businesses to put up prizes," someone suggested.

The warm room made Robin sleepy, and her mind wandered back to the lawyers. Today was rough, she thought, but what would it be like on a witness stand?

Robin turned sideways in the chair to get more comfortable and saw Pat Erickson sitting across the room in the back row. Troy was seated next to her, and Pat was whispering to him.

Now what's he trying to pull? Robin wondered. Pat had come down pretty heavy on drunk drivers on her radio commentaries. Was he trying to influence a reporter, trying to pull some strings? No, Pat's too smart for that—I hope.

Thirteen

"I never dreamed so many people would turn out for our Community Awareness Night," Robin said to Pat.

"You've all done such a great job." Pat gave Robin a little hug. "Honey, I can't tell you how proud I am of you and your friends."

Robin and Pat were sitting in folding chairs at the back of the auditorium. A table and a podium with a microphone were up front. Robin had opened the meeting, and Pat had given a talk. Then Robin had turned the rest of the program over to Mr. Whitmore, the Mayor of Woodbridge.

"I wish you'd tell me who your surprise speaker is," Robin said. "Is it a rock star or a pro football player or—"

Pat grinned. "Did anyone ever tell you that you don't have much patience?"

"Yes. Shane. He's always telling me." She

stopped and gave a long sigh.

"Ssh," Pat whispered, "Mr. Whitmore is about to introduce the speaker."

Full of excited anticipation, Robin leaned forward to see who would cross the auditorium and step up to the microphone. She knew Pat would pick someone special.

"Tonight's guest is a senior from Woodbridge High. I'd like to introduce Troy Haliburton."

Robin gasped. Stunned and angry, she turned on Pat. "How could you do this?" She got to her feet.

Pat held her arm. "Just sit down and listen, Robin."

"I'm not going to listen to excuses from him!"

"Please—stay for me."

"I don't know how you could do this, Pat." Robin sank down in the chair. She had missed Troy's first words.

He stood stiffly on the podium. His face was white and strained, and his voice shook slightly as if he were scared.

"Pat Erickson from station WBY asked me to come and talk to you tonight. Pat gave you some statistics about drunk driving, but one bears repeating. At sometime in our lives, one out of every two people will be involved in a drunk driving accident. ONE OUT OF EVERY TWO PEOPLE. Think about that for a minute. One out of every two."

Robin sat in stony silence, her arms folded, her face grim.

"Joining a group like SADD is the best thing that could happen to any teenager," Troy went on. "Nobody admits or even believes there's a big problem. But if we can change one night, one life, it's something."

He paused for a minute, then took the mike off the stand and moved off the podium. "I'm not here tonight to try to make you feel sorry for me."

Robin's jaw tightened.

"Believe me, I didn't want to come here. And I know there are a lot of you who'd rather not listen to what I have to say, but someone had to tell you about—that night.

"It was my birthday party—my eighteenth." He gave a grating little laugh. "That's when you're supposed to be old enough to have some sense. Right?" He shook his head. "I guess growing a year older doesn't mean you're any smarter.

"Anyway, somebody handed me a drink. I knew I was breaking training. But it was my birthday. How could one little drink hurt? After the first one, the second and third went down easily," Troy went on.

"Suddenly I realized I was supposed to have been home at four. It was late. 'So long, everybody,' I said. 'Thanks for the party.' "

Troy looked out over the audience. "I see a lot of people here tonight, but I don't see one friend who was at the party. Oh, I wouldn't have listened, not me, not the macho football star. No, I probably wouldn't have listened, but—not one of my friends tried to stop me.

"I got in my car, raced out of the driveway, and headed home. I put on my favorite tape and turned it up loud. I was singing away, feeling great, free, and easy behind the wheel.

"The street was shiny from the rain, and the streetlights made weird patterns on the pavement. The windshield wipers kept time to the music, going back and forth, back and forth— then the car skidded. I gripped the wheel. My foot was glued to the gas pedal. I should have been able to stop, but I felt as if my body belonged to somebody else."

Robin began to tremble. The car was coming toward her. She covered her mouth with her hands.

"I saw the two kids standing there by the bench. I saw them!" Troy's voice shook. "I saw them, but I couldn't stop!"

His head dropped and he stood there,

clenching his fists, a look of horror on his face.

Everyone in the room had stopped breathing.

His voice was a harsh whisper, "It's been six months, but that night will always be with me. I'd give anything to bring back that night—but I can't. I can't change anything, and that's what hurts. I can't even tell Shane I'm sorry.

"I am sorry, but that doesn't change anything for Shane.

"It's been a living hell for me, too. That night haunts me. I can't sleep. I wake up crying." His mouth twisted. "Oh, yes, the big tough guy can cry. I know I deserve whatever happens to me, but it's hard. The only kids who talk to me are the jerks who think it's smart to drink.

"I had to spend twenty-four hours in jail. I don't want to do that again—not ever! But the worst part is knowing I have to go through the rest of my life—remembering."

He put the mike back on the stand. There wasn't a sound in the auditorium. His voice carried clear to the back. "Don't feel sorry for me! Save your sympathy for the people who deserve it! At least I *can* remember." His voice broke. He blinked rapidly and wiped at his eyes with his arm. "But Shane—Shane may never remember anything ever again . . . ."

Troy walked through the silent crowd. As he passed Robin, their eyes met. Then he lowered his head and hurried on out.

Tears rolled down Robin's cheeks. "We're all losers," she whispered.

Pat took Robin in her arms. "Not losers, Robin. Victims. As long as anyone drinks and drives, no one wins."

* * * * *

The next morning Robin ran for a longer time than usual. There was so much to think about. One thing, sure, there were no easy answers. Pat was right, she thought, everyone's a victim—even Troy.

Her mind was a muddle, but at least the physical activity made her feel better.

She had no more than walked in the door when the phone rang. It was for her.

"Robin, come to the hospital right away," Shane's mother said excitedly. "Shane just opened his eyes. Hurry!"

Robin replaced the telephone and hurried into the living room where her parents were reading the Sunday paper.

"Mom? Dad? Shane opened his eyes! Will you take me to the hospital? He's going to get well. He's going to get well."

"Honey, that's the best news we've had in months," her mother said.

Her dad was putting on his shoes. "I was beginning to think this day would never come."

"Mom, would you call the kids and give them the good news?"

Her father laughed. "And shout it from the rooftop?"

Robin grinned. "No, I want to do that."

"Are you ready to go?" her father asked.

"Just as soon as I get Rabbit and my pink hat." She giggled. "I can't wait for him to see the hat on me."

On the way to the hospital, she could hardly sit still. "I'm so glad it's a beautiful day. It would have been crummy to wake up for the first time in months and see a gray sky. I kept telling everybody not to give up hope."

When they got to the hospital, her father asked if she wanted him to wait.

"No, that's okay, Dad. I'll ride home with Shane's parents."

As she was getting out of the car, her father leaned over and kissed her. "Honey, don't expect too much too soon."

"I won't, Dad." She waved and hurried into the hospital.

She smiled at the candy stripers with their

magazine carts. She nodded at the volunteer at the information desk. She resisted the urge to yell, "Shane's okay!"

All the elevators were in use. When she finally got on one, it seemed to take forever to get to Shane's floor.

Half expecting to find Shane sitting up in bed and drinking a milkshake, she practically flew into his room. His parents were sitting beside his bed.

Suddenly shy, she hesitated at the door. Shane was lying on his side facing away from her and she couldn't see his eyes.

"Hi," she whispered to his parents and grinned like an idiot. "Is he awake?"

She hurried around to the other side of the bed. His eyes were closed. He didn't look any different than he had for months.

"I'm so sorry, dear," Shane's mother said. "Sam told me not to call you, but I was so excited."

"Did he say anything?" Robin asked. "Did you tell him I was on my way? How long was he awake?"

"He wasn't really awake," Mr. McAllister said. Robin could hear the despair in his voice. "His eyes opened, but just rolled vacantly."

"But that's good, isn't it?" Robin asked, trying to hold on to the high spirits and optimism of a few minutes ago. "I mean, that has to be a sign that he's getting better."

"I don't know if it means anything," Mrs. McAllister said. "And I don't know how much more of this I can take."

Shane's mother burst into tears. Mr. McAllister put his arm around her and led her to the door. "You can't give up hope now, Margaret," he told his wife gently.

He turned and spoke to Robin. "I'm going to take her home. I'll come back and get you later."

"That's all right, Mr. McAllister. I'll call my dad."

Disappointment, like a heavy weight, made Robin's legs weak. She slumped down on the chair, still warm from Mrs. McAllister's body. Robin knew exactly how Shane's mother felt. The waiting, the not knowing were taking a toll on her, too.

She took Shane's hand and watched his face, willing his eyes to open.

"Shane McAllister, I know you can hear me. Now, you open your eyes and look at me," she commanded. "I've been really patient, and you know how rough that is for me. But I don't think you're trying hard enough. You wrote on my mirror that you loved me. Well, if you really do, you'll open your eyes or squeeze my hand. Give me some sign that you know I'm here." She tightened her grip on his hand. "I— I miss you so much . . . ."

She choked on the lump in her throat and blinked back the tears. "Come back, Shane. There's so much to do. I'll help you train. Did I tell you the track coach asked me to try out for the mile? I'm going to ask Cheryl to time me. I'm not as fast as you, but I have endurance."

She dug in her bag and pulled out Rabbit and set it on the bed beside Shane. "And this is what I'm going to wear." She put on the hat and tipped it at a cocky angle. "I hope you like it. You have to admit it's a pretty crazy hat. I may have to take off the feather or pin it down. Can't you just see it flying in the wind?" Her voice trembled. "I'll wear it every day if you'll just come back to me."

His eyelids fluttered. The movement was so slight she wasn't sure if she'd actually seen it.

"Shane? It's Robin, Shane."

Robin waited, her body tense, hardly breathing. The room was warm, and she felt the sweat break out in her palms. A siren wailed, bringing someone to emergency. The soft hush of nurses' shoes drifted in from the hall.

She took a long, quivering breath. "Shane?"

she whispered.

His lids fluttered, and this time she was sure.

"I'm right here," she breathed, not sure if she'd said the words aloud.

His eyes batted rapidly. His face was pale, then it turned dusky. He started to gasp, and his left arm and leg jerked.

"Shane!"

Frightened now, she jumped up and ran to the door. "Nurse! Something's wrong!"

The nurse hurried into the room to check on Shane. A sinking feeling hit Robin. It was like a weight on her chest as if she were drowning.

She heard the nurse whisper something like, "Oh, no! He's stopped breathing!" Robin found herself being propelled out of the room.

Over the loudspeaker, she heard, "Code Blue!"

Doctors and nurses with equipment rushed to Shane's room. People were running in and out.

Robin stood leaning against the wall. Numbness settled over her. She didn't feel a part of what was going on in Shane's room. Everything seemed far away. It was as if she were watching television with the sound turned down. She shivered. She was cold—so cold.

Then people were coming out of the room, one by one. It took a moment for her to realize that Dr. Webber was standing in front of her.

"I'm sorry, Robin. We did everything we could, but we couldn't save Shane."

The coldness turned to ice and spread through her body and around her heart. She began to shiver. "But he opened his eyes." Her voice didn't sound like her own. "He was getting better."

"When someone has been in a coma for five months, there are so many unexpected and unexplained complications. He could have developed a clot in his lung."

A nurse came up and put her arms around Robin. "I've called Shane's parents and yours. Come into the nurses' lounge to wait."

Robin shook her head and looked at the doctor. "May I see him?"

"Yes," he said, then searched her face. "But are you all right? Do you want someone with you?"

Robin shook her head. "I just want to tell him good-bye."

Her body felt cold and stiff as she went into his room and sat beside the bed. He looked so peaceful, but so still, so very still.

"I'm wearing my hat, Shane. I don't care if everybody laughs at it. I love it."

She looked around for Rabbit. The little stuffed animal had somehow fallen under the bed. Robin retrieved it and held it to her cheek. "We're both going to miss you, you know."

An icy, burning tear dropped on Rabbit's face. Gently, she placed Rabbit in the curve of Shane's arm and whispered, "Old MacDonald had a farm. Ee—ay—ee—ay—oh. . . ."

A note from Robert Anastas, founder of SADD

When I began SADD in 1981 there were over 6,200 young people dying on our highways because of drinking and driving. I have criss-crossed this country for five years unmasking death and asking young people to join with me and eliminate this senseless tragedy.

The youth of America have responded to the challenge and reduced the carnage on our highways by almost two thirds. The National Highway Traffic Safety Administration announced that the figure for 1985 for young people ages 15 through 19 killed by drinking and driving was 2,130. Our goal is to eliminate all deaths on our highways due to drinking and driving.

We began with one SADD chapter in Wayland, Massachusetts, and today there are over 10,000 high school chapters, 3,000 junior high chapters, and 300 college chapters throughout the United States, Canada, Australia, New Zealand, and Europe. I am proud of the youth who have responded to the cause. They really believe as I do that the best of life is yet to be.